"I gather you want to talk."

Nik spun back to her with the liquid grace of movement that always caught her eye, and frowned at her, black brows drawing down, wide sensual mouth twisting in dismissal.

"No. I don't want to talk," he told Betsy abruptly before he tossed back the finger of Scots whiskey he had poured neat and set the empty glass down again.

"Then *why*—?" she began in confusion.

"*Se thelo*...I want you," he heard himself admit before he was even aware that the words were on his tongue.

So Nik, *so* explosively unpredictable, Betsy reasoned abstractedly, color rushing into her cheeks as a hot wave of awareness engulfed her. Jewel-bright eyes assailed hers in an almost physical collision, and something low and intimate in her body twisted hard. Her legs turned so weak she wasn't convinced they were still there to hold her up, but she was held in stasis by the intensity of his narrowed green gaze.

"And you want me," he told her thickly.

The Legacies of Powerful Men

Three tenets to live by: money, power and the ruthless pursuit of passion!

Cristo Ravelli, Nik Christakis and Zarif al-Rastani know better than most the double-edged sword of their inheritance. Watching their father move from one wife to another, leaving their mothers devastated in his wake, has hardened each of these men against the lure of love.

But despite their best efforts to live by the three tenets of money, power and passion, they find themselves entangled with three women who challenge the one thing that they've protected all these years.

Their hearts!

Read Cristo's story in:

Ravelli's Defiant Bride

June 2014

Read Nik's story in:

Christakis's Rebellious Wife

July 2014

And read Zarif's story in:

Zarif's Convenient Queen

August 2014

Lynne Graham

—

Christakis's Rebellious Wife

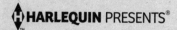
HARLEQUIN PRESENTS®

Recycling programs
for this product may
not exist in your area.

ISBN-13: 978-0-373-13256-0

CHRISTAKIS'S REBELLIOUS WIFE

First North American Publication 2014

Copyright © 2014 by Lynne Graham

This edition published by arrangement with Harlequin Books S.A.

For questions and comments about the quality of this book,
please contact us at CustomerService@Harlequin.com.

Printed in U.S.A.

All about the author...
Lynne Graham

Born of Irish/Scottish parentage, **LYNNE GRAHAM** has lived in Northern Ireland all her life. She has one brother. She grew up in a seaside village and now lives in a country house surrounded by a woodland garden, which is wonderfully private.

Lynne first met her husband when she was fourteen. They married after she completed a degree at Edinburgh University. Lynne wrote her first book at fifteen—it was rejected everywhere. She started writing again when she was at home with her first child. It took several attempts before she was published, and she has never forgotten the delight of seeing that first book for sale at the local newsagents.

Lynne always wanted a large family, and she now has five children. Her eldest, her only natural child, is in her twenties and is a university graduate. Her other children, who are every bit as dear to her heart, are adopted: two from Sri Lanka and two from Guatemala. In Lynne's home, there is a rich and diverse cultural mix, which adds a whole extra dimension of interest and discovery to family life.

The family has two pets. Thomas, a very large and affectionate black cat, bosses the dog and hunts rabbits. The dog is Daisy, an adorable but not very bright white West Highland terrier, who loves being chased by the cat. At night, dog and cat sleep together in front of the kitchen stove.

Lynne loves gardening, cooking, collects everything from old toys to rock specimens, and is crazy about every aspect of Christmas.

Other titles by Lynne Graham available in ebook:

RAVELLI'S DEFIANT BRIDE *(The Legacies of Powerful Men)*
THE DIMITRAKOS PROPOSITION
CHALLENGING DANTE *(A Bride for a Billionaire)*
THE BILLIONAIRE'S TROPHY *(A Bride for a Billionaire)*

To my daughter Rachel with warm appreciation
for all her support.

CHAPTER ONE

'A DIVORCE CAN be civilised,' Cristo Ravelli pronounced in a tone of studious tact.

Nik Christakis almost vented a derisive laugh at such a statement from the brother barely two months his senior. In reality only genuine respect for his sibling kept his cutting tongue silent. After all, what could Cristo possibly know about the blood and mayhem of a bitter divorce? Cristo was a newly and very happily married man without that experience…or that of many other unpleasant life events, in Nik's considered opinion. As a result, Cristo was as solid and straight as a ruler; he had no corners, no twists, no hidden places. He had no more concept of Nik's infinitely more complex and darker life experience than a dinosaur catapulted into a fairy story full of fluffy wings and magic.

'I know you're probably wondering where I get the nerve to offer advice,' Cristo remarked shrewdly. 'But you and Betsy did once have a good relationship and ratcheting down the current tension and cooling the aggro would be healthier for both of you—'

'Then you should be delighted to hear that Betsy and I are having a face-to-face meeting tomorrow in the presence of our lawyers in an effort to iron out a settlement,' Nik growled, his lean, darkly handsome features grim and hard.

'It's only money, Nik, and… *Dio mio…*' Cristo sighed, thinking wryly of the vast business empire that his workaholic tycoon brother had built from the ground up '…you have plenty of it—'

Nik ground his perfect white teeth together, his unusually light green eyes flashing bright with barely restrained fury. 'That's not the point!' he cut in harshly. 'Betsy's trying to take me to the cleaners and steal half of everything I have—'

'I can't explain why she's making such excessive demands. I would've sworn she didn't have a mercenary bone in her body,' Cristo fielded uncomfortably. 'Have you tried to talk to her, Nik?'

Nik frowned darkly. 'Why would I try to *talk* to her?' he asked in astonishment at a suggestion that clearly struck him as insane. 'She threw me out of our home, started a divorce and is currently trying to rip me off to the tune of billions!'

'She did have some excuse for throwing you out,' Cristo reminded his sibling in a rueful undertone.

In answer, Nik compressed his lips. He had his own very firm ideas about exactly why his marriage had imploded. He had married a woman who said she didn't want children and then she had *changed her mind*. It was true that he had chosen to withhold certain very private information from her in the aftermath of that revelation but he had understandably assumed that her change of heart was a whim or at best hormonal, an urge that might hopefully fade as quickly as it had first arrived.

'It was *my* house,' Nik responded flatly.

'So now you're planning to take Lavender Hall off her as well as the dog,' Cristo breathed heavily.

'Gizmo was *also* mine.' Nik glanced at the disputed dog, returned to his care two months earlier and still a study of deep doggy depression. Gizmo slumped by the window, an array of squeaky toys lying around him untouched, his short muzzle resting mournfully on shaggy paws. The animal had the best of everything that money could buy but, in spite of Nik's every effort to the contrary, the wretched mutt continued to pine for Betsy.

'Have you any idea how devastated she was when you took the dog off her?' Cristo enquired.

'The three pages of tear-stained care instructions that came with him did provide a hint,' Nik breathed sardonically. 'She was more worried about the dog than she ever was about me—'

'Less than a year ago, Betsy *adored* you!' Cristo shot back at his brother in condemnation of that unfeeling response.

And he had liked being adored, Nik acknowledged; he had liked it very much indeed. When adoration had turned to violent hatred and questions he couldn't answer he had had no appetite whatsoever for the new regime. Questions he *could* have answered had he been forced to do so, he qualified inwardly, but he could not have stood to see the look of pity or horror on her face should he have told her the truth. Some truths a man was entitled to keep private; some were simply too appalling to share.

'I mean…' Cristo hesitated. 'When you encouraged me to talk to Betsy, to become her friend after you split, I thought it was because you loved her and wanted her back and hoped to use me as an intermediary—'

Nik's devastatingly handsome face clenched hard. 'I didn't love her. I've never loved anyone,' he admitted coldly. 'I liked her, *trusted* her. She was a good homemaker—'

'A…*homemaker?*' Cristo was staggered by that description because it was such an old-fashioned term and there was nothing even remotely old-fashioned about Nik and his brand of contemporary cool.

'A good homemaker,' Nik repeated steadily, guessing that Cristo, who had always had a decent home, could not comprehend the draw of such a talent in a woman. 'But my trust in her was misplaced and obviously I don't want her back.'

'Are you absolutely certain of that?' Cristo pressed.

'*Ne*…yes,' Nik confirmed in Greek, his response instantaneous. He might not be divorced as yet but he had already moved on. After all, Betsy had always been an eccentric choice of bride for a Greek billionaire but she had appeared during a troubled period in his life and she belonged to that phase, most assuredly not to the new start and more promising future he now envisaged. In the space of the six months that had passed since their marriage broke down, Nik had changed and he was very proud of that change. He had shed his dysfunctional past, travelled from being a male with more excess baggage than a jumbo jet to a faster-moving, far more efficient version of himself. The very last thing he intended to do now was repeat past mistakes. And Betsy had been a *serious* mistake.

No matter how hard Betsy tried to hide it, she was so much on edge in the company of her polished legal team while they waited in the elegant conference room that a sudden noise would have seen her plastered to the ceiling.

Her nervous tension was understandable. After all, it had been six months since she had last seen Nik, six months during which her already broken heart had been repeatedly stamped on and then what little remained torn to pieces. He had refused to see her or make any explanation for his extraordinary behaviour. In the space of a moment she had travelled from being a happily married woman trying for her first baby to a betrayed, bitterly hurt and confused wife.

She had thrown Nik out but *he* had essentially abandoned *her*. After his heartless deception, the force of his counter-attack had almost destroyed her and he had walked away without a backward glance. He had reacted as if three years of marriage, and what she had honestly assumed was happiness, meant absolutely nothing to him. Too late had it occurred to her that she had married a man who had never said he loved her, who had said in fact that he didn't believe in love and who at all times and on all occasions had made his business affairs, rather than her, the top priority in his life.

So, after that shattering betrayal of trust and his very final rejection, it was hardly a surprise that she was finally hitting back. And she knew this course of action would take his feelings towards her from apparent indifference to actively *hating* her. And she didn't care; no, she definitely didn't care what Nikolos Christakis thought of her any more. Love had died when she was finally forced to acknowledge the degradingly low value he had set on her and their marriage, and she supposed that what she was now engaged in was a rather pathetic attempt at hitting back to punish him for the heartbreak he had callously inflicted.

Revenge. It was not a pretty or feminine word but it was also the very last thing a manipulative and cunning business shark like Nik Christakis would expect from his once submissive and soon-to-be ex-wife. He hadn't cared about her but he *did* care about his precious money. There was no greater goal in Nik's life than the ruthless pursuit of profit and the clever conservation of that vast store of personal wealth. Betsy knew that if she could significantly dent Nik in the wallet department, if in no other way, she would finally draw blood. After all, it had taken her outrageous claim of half of everything he possessed to persuade Nik into an actual face-to-face meeting with her again. Self-evidently money mattered to Nik more than she or their marriage had ever mattered.

Footsteps sounded in the corridor outside and

Betsy stiffened. The door handle made a slight noise but the door stayed shut and she froze, her heart leaping into her mouth.

'Let us do the talking,' her legal representative, Stewart Annersley, reminded her afresh.

He might as easily have said that Betsy was out of her league in such company but she already knew that, could barely credit that she had spent three entire years in Nik's world of rarefied wealth and yet contrived to remain easily shocked and gullible. What did that say about her? Was she stupid? A poor reader of people and their motivations? She had been distraught when Nik had taken Gizmo from her. The little dog had been her only comfort and even though Nik was by no means a doggy-orientated male, he had still insisted on taking the animal back. Why?

Betsy believed it was because Nik was the ultimate control freak. Evidently, what was his *stayed* his, unless it was a discarded wife. His most recent attack had been to go after the house that he had never liked but that she loved. Why? Certainly he owned it and he had paid for the restoration, yet he had only bought the property to please her. Or *had* he? Had he simply seen Lavender Hall as a promising investment? More and more Betsy doubted the assumptions she had once made about what motivated Nik.

Without warning, the door sprang open and framed Nik's very tall, well-built body. Her heart hammered madly for a split second and then felt as though it had stopped beating altogether because for a long timeless moment she couldn't move, couldn't breathe, couldn't speak, couldn't even blink. He radiated raw sexual charisma.

His extraordinarily light eyes glittered like gleaming emeralds in his lean, darkly beautiful face, startlingly noticeable eyes and shockingly astute. A thousand memories threatened to consume her—from the recollection of their disastrous first date to their idyllic honeymoon and the lonely challenge of her life once reality had set in—and she fought them off fiercely. He wasn't going to do this to her again, she swore with inner vehemence. He *wasn't* going to break her nerve again.

She lifted her chin, squared her stiff shoulders and stared back at him while carefully blanking him out because she could not face direct eye contact. Yet in the back of her mind she was still plunged into sudden agony by his presence, wondering how this had happened to them, how the man she had once adored could have become her worst enemy. Where had she gone wrong? What had she done to make him treat her with such hostility and unkindness?

And even while paranoia and self-pity threatened to overwhelm Betsy for a dangerous instant, it was Nik's voice she heard inside her head. *'Stop with the persecution complex and the blame game,'* he had once told her. *'Not everything's your fault. You're not being punished for some sin in this world or the next. The bad stuff is simply what life throws at you...'*

Nik scanned Betsy with compulsive intensity. Had she shrunk? She had never been very big in either height or size—indeed she barely weighed a hundred pounds soaking wet. Surrounded by her legal posse she was utterly overshadowed. She had definitely lost weight. He wondered if she was eating properly, an old protective instinct kicking in, instantly stamped down on hard and consigned to the back of his mind as inappropriate. It was none of his business any more, equally none of his business that her lawyer, Annersley, was leaning far too close to her, appreciative eyes pinned to Betsy's delicate profile as if she were a prize up for grabs. And of course, endowed with even a tithe of what Nik was worth, Betsy would be very much a trophy for some scheming male to snatch up in the future.

That idea didn't bother Nik, no, it didn't bother him at all, he told himself fiercely, sliding with a degree of unnecessary force into the chair spun out for him by his own team. Naturally there would be other men in Betsy's future; she was a beauty. His attention skimmed over her pale profile. She had always reminded him of a spun-glass figurine, fragile in every proportion, the sort of woman a man wanted to protect and cherish. And where had that chivalrous attitude, shown only to her, taken him? he asked himself cynically. On the road to the divorce court and a poorer future like a thousand other foolish men. *'I want a baby,'* she had said, all tearful blue eyes and trembling lips, breaking their premarital agreement, trying to selfishly, wilfully rewrite history... And she hadn't even noticed that the bottom had fallen out of his world the moment she spoke.

Obviously, Betsy would have that much-desired

baby with another man now. Without warning, Nik's stomach lurched. He gulped down the cup of hot black coffee offered to him and burnt his mouth. Betsy was trying to rob him blind just as his gigolo father, Gaetano, had once tried to rob Nik's mother, Helena. Helena Christakis, however, had been too clever to be conned by Gaetano Ravelli, and Nik's IQ left his mother's at the starting stakes.

More to the point, he didn't give a damn about Betsy now. Like an alcoholic he was taking the cure and the cure was *seeing* her again and feeling nothing. And there she was: tiny, exquisitely provocative in every detail from her cloak of silky pale blonde hair and porcelain skin to the luscious pout of her naturally pink lips. Hard jawline squaring, he searched out her flaws and underlined them in his head: the bump in her nose, the faint scattering of freckles, the ridiculous lack of height and the very modest curves. On a physical level she was very far from being perfect... What the hell had he ever seen in her?

Without warning Betsy glanced up, soft feathery lashes lifting to reveal eyes the colour of the deepest ocean, and instantaneous lust gripped Nik in an iron fist, punching through him so fast that his big, powerful body tensed, his muscles pulling defensively taut while the hungry swelling at his groin tightened the sleek fit of his tailored trousers. His response shocked him and it took a great deal to shock Nik. Indeed, the consternation that followed made sweat break out on his upper lip before he turned colder than snow, utilising every fibre of his single-minded character to crush his unwelcome response to her. Obviously, he reasoned grimly, his momentary arousal was nothing more complex than the knee-jerk reaction of an old habit around a sexually familiar woman.

Betsy stared fixedly at the table while the legal formalities got under way. Nik was at the far end, distant enough to be visually ignored, but every strand of her being was working against her will to turn her neck in that direction to snatch a glance at him. It had been so long, so agonisingly long since she had had the simple luxury of looking at him. Some instinct she could not suppress lifted her head up and for one explosive split second of time she collided with Nik's stunning green eyes, eyes that were positively startling in that lean, dark, devastatingly handsome face of his.

Suddenly she couldn't breathe or move again and the most primitive responses controlled her. Molten heat surged at the core of her and she literally *felt* her breasts stir inside her bra, her nipples prickling and straining into swollen buds. A welter of erotic images assailed her and burning colour drove off her pallor. Later it would hurt that Nik had the power to look away first but in the instant that disconnection occurred she was merely grateful to be set free of that terrible awareness and craving again. How could he still do that to her? How could she *still* feel the power of his scorching sexual attraction?

After all, Nik had put her through hell. He had stayed silent when he should have spoken up. He had even allowed her to go through the horrendous humiliation of discovering the truth that had made a mockery of their marriage from the lips of one of his brothers.

'You will regret this...' Nik had warned her forbiddingly the day she had thrown him out, but her sole regret then had been that she had not found out what he had been hiding from her sooner.

In retrospect she knew she had behaved like a madwoman that day. Temporary insanity had gripped her from the minute her whole world came crashing down around her. She had screamed, she had shouted, she had cursed and he had stood there like a granite rock battered by stormy seas—essentially untouched by her anger, her tears and her pleas for an explanation. In fact he had said nothing beyond the quiet, unemotional admission that what she had learned about him from his younger brother Zarif was indeed the truth: Nik had had a vasectomy at the age of twenty-two and there was absolutely no possibility of him ever having a child with her. But Nik had excluded Betsy from that secret and, unforgivably, he had allowed her to break her heart trying and failing to get pregnant for months on end. Why hadn't he just told her the truth? *'Why?'* she had demanded again and again, and he had stared back at her in resolute brooding silence, refusing to explain his behaviour.

Marisa Glover, the celebrated divorce lawyer by Nik's side, studied Betsy with cool blue eyes and quite casually asked her why she believed that a woman who had been a penniless, dyslexic waitress before her marriage and had not worked since should have a legal claim on half her husband's estate.

'Let's face it…you have no children to support,' the icy blonde beauty reminded the table at large.

All of a sudden, Betsy was bone-white and reeling from the stream of virtual body blows landing on her with the devastating efficiency of bombs, her skin squeezing tight over her bones in horror. Nik had *told* them; he had told them she was dyslexic and mortification drenched her like icy water thrown in her face. As for the reminder that she had no children, that was an even more cruel strike considering that Nik had comprehensively and deviously denied her what she had so desperately wanted.

Her lawyer stepped in to steer the topic in a more practical direction.

Nik scrutinised Betsy's pale, taut profile, the anxious flicker of her lashes, the tightness of her lips, and knew she was hurt, humiliated and still recoiling from Marisa's opening salvo. Marisa was the best divorce lawyer in London and an unashamed barracuda and Nik always employed the best. But now his perfect white teeth were gritted, brown fingers clenching into a fist against a long, powerful thigh. Had Betsy expected him to play nice? Had she thought anything could still be sacred, that anything could remain a secret in their divorce? Could she still be that innocent?

He was still waiting for her legal team to attack, for they certainly had the ammunition. It went without saying that he did not want the curious facts of his hush-hush vasectomy aired in an open court. That was private, considerably more so in his opinion than the dyslexia she was so ashamed of suffering from.

Even so the shaken look of pain and betrayal etched in her tightly controlled but oh, so expressive face got to him whether he liked it or not and distaste and impatience rose in Nik for degrading Betsy in front of witnesses.

Annersley was currently engaged in reminding Marisa that Nik had refused to allow Betsy to work during their marriage, implying that Nik was a dinosaur and a bully of no mean order but doing so in the politest of terms. Marisa was pointing out that Betsy lacked the education required to gain anything other than the most menial of jobs and that a man of Nik's social status could hardly be expected to tolerate a wife taking an unskilled, humble position.

Something suddenly snapped Nik's hold on his volatile temper. Without even thinking about what he was doing, he ground his hands down on the edge of the conference table and sprang upright with an abruptness that startled everybody present. Lean, strong face hawklike, he growled, '*Diavelos*...enough! This ends here. Marisa, you are well aware that Betsy single-handedly runs her own business at Lavender Hall—'

'Well, yes, *but*—'

'We are finished here for now,' he ground out with harsh finality. 'I will discuss this no further—'

'But nothing's been agreed,' Annersley complained.

Betsy stole a grudging glance at Nik, scarcely able to credit that he had brought the humiliating session to so swift a halt. Surely he could not have done that for *her* benefit? She refused to believe that; he had to have some clever ulterior motive. She felt wounded and degraded after having her dyslexia thrown in her face, not to mention the reminder that she had never completed her education to an acceptable level. It infuriated her that she could blame Nik for that last reality, for Nik had complained so bitterly when she was attending evening classes to study for her A levels that she had eventually given them up. Nik might have travelled the globe constantly during their marriage, but when he was at home he had made it very, very clear to her that he always expected her to be there. And she had finally given way to his selfish protests, naively believing that he was admitting to *needing* her and secretly gratified that the male who did not tell her he loved her could not bear to find her missing or unavailable.

'There will be another meeting,' Nik decreed, striding to the door without another glance in Betsy's direction.

Betsy got off the train and walked to her car.

She was angry with herself, as angry as she was ashamed that she had reacted to Nik on so basic a level, responding to his lethal sexual attraction like a silly young girl without self-knowledge or defences. She wanted to feel nothing, absolutely nothing around Nik. After all, nothing was what he deserved. Cristo's wife, Belle, had told Betsy that she should be dating again and that she would not get past her experience with Nik until she did. Unfortunately the last thing

Betsy needed after the heart-rending grief of her marriage breakdown was another man to worry about. Men were very high maintenance; Nik had taught her that.

Her troubled thoughts were already whisking her back in time. When she had first met Nik Christakis she had been working as a waitress at a little bistro across the road from his office.

She had enjoyed her job. *'If a job's worth doing, it's worth doing well,'* her late grandmother had told her when she was a child, and the truth of that homely maxim had never let Betsy down. She refused to let the fact that a job was humble or low paid colour her attitude, but she had always known that had her grandmother survived she would have been very disappointed by Betsy's lack of educational achievement. Her loving gran had taught her that with extra time and specialised tutoring she could overcome her dyslexia and that it was not an excuse for low expectations in life. That awareness in mind, she had chosen her job to fit the fact that she was studying several nights a week at evening class to get her A levels. Oh, she'd had *big* plans back then for a more promising future.

In those days it had never occurred to her that a man could come between her and her wits. She was twenty-one and boys had come and gone, but nobody special, nobody capable of engaging her heart or tempting her body. When she had first seen Nik, he had been sitting at one of her tables in the spring sunshine: a stunningly beautiful male sheathed in a black cashmere overcoat, light green eyes framed by impossibly long, lush black lashes, zapping her with instant tingling awareness as he ordered coffee. She hadn't noticed that Cristo was with him that first time, hadn't even registered the presence of plain-suited men by the wall, hovering with the protectiveness of bodyguards. As always Nik had commanded full centre stage. Her heart had beat so fast it had felt as if it were in her throat and she had feared its crazy acceleration would choke her.

When he had ordered a second coffee, she had left a complimentary biscuit on the table but he had handed it back to her. 'I don't touch sugar…*ever,*' he had told her softly, his foreign accent purring along the syllables with disturbing sexiness.

'Wish I could say the same,' Betsy had breezed back, popping the biscuit in her pocket for later. She had always been hungry, free meals or snacks not having been part of her employment terms. 'But I still have to bring you the biscuit with your coffee. It's management policy.'

'Wasteful,' he had pronounced with a sardonic curve to his handsome mouth. 'But you look like you could use the calories.'

'I'm just skinny. I've always been skinny,' Betsy had parried, dimly conscious of his companion's frowning, silent scrutiny.

'*Cute* skinny,' Nik had countered, whipping his keen gaze over her slender proportions, sending colour flying like a banner into her cheeks. 'Very, *very* cute.'

And she had rushed away to get that second coffee, wondering what on earth was wrong with her. He hadn't been the first customer to try to flirt with her and she had usually taken it in her stride as simple banter, infinitely preferring that approach to that of the occasional creeps who had let their hands stray if she'd got too close. It hadn't occurred to her that he might have actually meant anything by his remarks. After all, she had noticed his fancy coat and the sleek dark suit he had worn beneath it and already categorised him as some high-flying city-executive type and, as such, completely out of her league.

The next time she had served him he had offered her the biscuit first and she had flushed and said hurriedly, 'No, thanks. My boss told me we're not allowed to eat the biscuits because it looks bad.'

'Really?' Nik had quirked a black brow. 'Maybe I should have a word with him—'

'No, please don't say anything,' Betsy had urged in harried retreat with her tray.

'If it worries you that much I won't. My name's Nik, by the way,' he had responded casually.

A tin of incredibly expensive fancy biscuits had been delivered to her at work that afternoon, the gift card signed with a slashed 'Nik'. Betsy had been more embarrassed than pleased, particularly when her boss, Mark, had noted the delivery, asked her if the gift was from a customer and frowned in disapproval when she had confirmed it. When she had thanked Nik for the gift he had shrugged it off as if it was too unimportant to mention.

Nik had come in every Tuesday after that, settling down to chat in a foreign language to Cristo while constantly fielding calls on his mobile phone. Just seeing him had thrilled her and meeting his eyes had electrified her all over, sending heat laced with weird chills racing through her body in an uncontrollable surge. It had not escaped her notice that he watched her as well and that he left her ridiculously large tips that swelled the staff collection box as never before.

'Be careful around that guy,' Mark had warned her one morning. 'I've only just realised who he is. He's Nik Christakis and he owns the office block opposite—NCI, Nik Christakis Industries. And guess what? In his no-doubt vast portfolio of businesses he already has a large chain of coffee shops and I wouldn't like to get on the wrong side of him.'

'He *owns* the building over there?' Betsy had gasped.

'Haven't you ever noticed his bodyguards?' Mark had rolled his eyes at her lack of observation. 'He has to be an extraordinarily wealthy man to need security and you do have to wonder why he's slumming here with us.'

Betsy had felt foolish for not appreciating that Nik was as much a fish out of water in the bistro as snow in July. She had looked him up online and learned that he was Greek and that Cristo was his half-brother. She'd also discovered that Nik had grown up in a very different world from her own. Embarrassed by the adolescent daydreams she had been weaving round

him until that point, she had become more circum-
spect in her behaviour when he was around.

'No smile for me?' Nik had queried on his next
visit, catching her fingers in his to halt her and
sharply disconcerting her with that move. 'Is something wrong?'

Azure eyes wide, she had reddened. 'No, nothing's
wrong. We're just very busy and I'm a bit distracted.'

'Have dinner with me tomorrow night,' Nik had
drawled without warning.

Jolted by the invitation, and scarcely believing that
he was serious, Betsy had jerkily retrieved her fingers and clutched at her tray. 'Sorry, I can't. I've got
a class—'

'The next night you're free,' Nik had interposed
smoothly.

'We've got nothing in common,' she had protested.

'But I want you because you're different,' Nik had
informed her huskily, making her drop her eyes in
shock at that blunt admission and shiver as though
her insides were being subjected to a force-ten gale.

'It wouldn't work,' she had argued in a low voice.

'If I say it will work, it will work. *When?*' Nik had
pressed mercilessly.

'Er...Friday,' she had admitted in the suffocating
silence, horrendously aware of his brother's incredulous scrutiny. 'I'm free Friday night.'

'I'll pick you up at half eight,' Nik had responded
calmly and asked for her address.

As she had moved away to serve another customer
she had heard Cristo arguing with his brother and she

had just *known* it was about her and that Nik's sibling could not credit that his brother had invited a waitress out on a date.

Nik had steamrollered over her objections and she should have seen the writing on the wall then. Nik didn't quit until he got what he wanted. He was relentless, unstoppable and stubborn as a mule.

CHAPTER TWO

NIK WAS ENSCONCED in his limo with a very beautiful blonde. Jenna had seemed the perfect antidote to his difficult morning. She was light-hearted and fun and she wasn't looking for anything serious. She had invited him back to her apartment and neither of them had any illusion about what was to happen there. Now she snuggled up against him, her hand fastening possessively to a long, powerful thigh. He stiffened, resisting a strong urge to shake her off. He was getting a divorce, he reminded himself obstinately. He was a free man. It was past time he acted on that change of status.

Jenna shifted almost onto his lap to kiss him. In a defensive move, he threw his head back and her lips caught his jawline instead. The scent of her washed over him and she smelled wrong to him. Not bad, just somehow and inexplicably…*wrong*. He lifted a hand to her shoulder, long fingers accidentally brushing her hair. It felt coarse instead of silky and he didn't want to touch it. In a fury he willed himself to stop making crazy comparisons. Maybe that was why the normal, healthy male response to an approach from a willing, attractive woman wasn't happening for him.

Thee mou...his body was demonstrating all the re-action of a solid block of wood, he acknowledged in mounting frustration. Something was messing with his head and his libido and he didn't know what but neither was he prepared to discuss the problem with his therapist. He had been forced to explore quite enough unpleasant issues with the good doctor and, while he had every respect for the lady's common sense and discretion, there were still some things he refused to share. He might have unburdened himself of the dark weight of his dysfunctional past and felt stronger for it, but the freedom to return to his former taciturn habits was equally a relief. Sharing anything did not come naturally to a male with his reserved nature. And such acknowledgements were only one more unnecessary reminder that being involved in any way with Betsy was still ruining his life, cutting off his choices and reminding him of his boundaries while stifling the raw energy, the voracious sex drive and the sheer ruthlessness that had always healthily compelled Nik forward in life.

His mobile phone buzzed and he dug it out with an apology, but he already knew he wasn't going back to Jenna's apartment. Clearly she didn't attract him enough, he reflected grimly. When he added in the unthinkable, that for the first time in his life he might fail between the sheets, it was sufficient to crush his need to test himself and prove that he had left his marriage behind him.

No, to achieve that goal he required a rather more civilised approach, he conceded broodingly, momentarily forgetting his companion. Taking some of the aggro out of the situation between him and Betsy would be a good strategic move. That didn't mean he was going to give her a cartload of money or grant any of her ridiculous requests or, worse still, *talk* to her as Cristo had so ludicrously suggested. He didn't want to talk to Betsy. He wouldn't keep his temper if he talked to her and any gain from his breaking of the ice between them would be swiftly destroyed by a fresh flood of hostility and mutual resentment. No, talking of any kind was off the table. *Diavelos,* the lawyers could do the talking.

The day after the legal meeting, Betsy set out the items for sale on the new shelves in the shop and stepped back to assess the display.

She might have gone through hell since her marriage had broken down but, when it came to work, her overwhelming need to keep busy and mentally challenged had ironically ensured that the same months were astonishingly productive and creative in business terms. The little farm shop selling fresh veg, fruit and eggs, which Nik had grudgingly allowed her to open in one of the redundant farm buildings behind the hall, had tripled in size to house the baked goods and home-cooked ready meals she had sourced. Since then she had added the card and gift section, where she stocked everything from potpourri to local crafts. Across the yard, work was noisily progressing as a former ruined cottage was transformed into a small coffee shop.

Behind the counter, her manager, Alice, was chatting cheerfully to a regular customer stocking up for her weekly shop. Betsy had initially hired Alice to ensure that she was always available when Nik was at home, but even though she was now able to work much longer hours the arrangement still worked well. After all, the business had expanded and Alice was good at dealing with the financial side of things, while Betsy was happiest handling suppliers and sourcing new goods.

Furthermore, Alice had the wisdom to understand when not to ask awkward questions. Divorced from a cheating ex and raising three children, she knew all about sleepless nights and heartache. Alice had not said a word when she came into work some mornings and found all their produce rearranged, the fruit so shiny it looked polished and the tiled floor so clean you could see your face in it. Time after time Betsy had taken refuge in work when she couldn't sleep. But there was a far more practical reason behind her industry and the long hours she put in.

Betsy's ultimate goal was to make Lavender Hall self-sufficient because she was mortified by the prospect of hanging on Nik's sleeve for the rest of her days. If she built up the business enough it could support her and cover the wages bill for the staff required not only to run the business but also to maintain the house and garden. In truth, claiming a very large slice of Nik's fortune had not solely been an act of aggression or revenge but more of a counter-attack to his unreasonable demand that Lavender Hall be sold. The house offered Betsy an unparalleled resource as a business base from which she could earn her own living and she had lots of even more ambitious ideas on the back burner for the future.

The phone on the counter buzzed and Alice answered it. 'It's for you,' she told Betsy.

Edna, the hall housekeeper, was on the line. 'You have a visitor, Mrs Christakis. Is it still all right for me to take the afternoon off?' the older woman asked anxiously.

Edna and her husband, Stan, who kept the garden, had provided sterling ongoing support on the home front after Betsy had had to cut back on staff after Nik's departure. With Nik and his high expectations of instant service removed from the equation, there had been no need for a fancy private chef, a driver or a flock of maids.

'Of course it is,' Betsy assured her while abstractedly wondering why she had not named the visitor. Obviously someone familiar, possibly Cristo or even his wife, Belle, she thought hopefully, because she was in the mood for some uplifting company.

Betsy liked Belle, a leggy Irish redhead with boundless vitality and a great sense of fun. Belle had slowly become a trusted friend in spite of the fact that what Belle had to say about Nik was pretty much unrepeatable. Betsy, in turn, admired the way Belle and Cristo had taken on responsibility for the five kids Belle's mother had had during her long-running affair with Cristo and Nik's late father, Gaetano. Nik would never have sacrificed his personal freedom on such a score, she conceded painfully, wondering how she had contrived to be so blind to the reality that the man she wanted to father her child didn't even *like* children.

Smoothing her stretchy black skirt down over her hips and twitching down the pushed-up sleeves of her pink honeycomb-knit sweater, Betsy left the shop and cut through the walled garden to the door in the ten-foot wall that led straight into the hall's vast rear courtyard. When Nik had protested her desire for a commercial outlet at their home, she had reminded him of the size of that wall and had added that the opening up of the former farm lane would preserve their privacy from both customers and traffic. He had remained stalwartly unimpressed, giving way solely because he had known she needed something to occupy her while he travelled abroad so much.

And yet now here she was, running not the hobby shop *he* had envisaged but her own thriving business, she reflected ruefully, striving to raise her flagging spirits with that comforting reminder. Who would ever have thought she had that capability? Certainly not her parents, who had never expected much from her. It had been her grandmother, a retired teacher, who had ensured that Betsy got the help she needed with her dyslexia. In truth, Betsy's parents had never really had much time for Betsy and had been ashamed of her reading and writing difficulties. In fact she was convinced that she had been an accidental conception because even as a child she had been aware that her parents resented the incessant demands of parenthood, no matter how much her grandmother tried to help them out. Her parents had died in a train crash when Betsy was eleven. By then her grandmother had already passed away and Betsy had had to go into foster care, the first seed of her conviction that she would never ever want children already sown by her own distinctly chilly upbringing.

Cutting through the spacious empty kitchen, Betsy hurried through to the big hall and came to a startled halt when she saw the tall, broad-shouldered male with blacker than black hair, standing poised with his back turned to her by the still-open front door.

Nik had already surveyed his surroundings with keen interest, instantly noting the changes since his exit six months earlier. The furniture was a little dusty. There were no fresh flowers adorning the central table, not even a welcoming fire burning in the massive grate. But superimposed over that picture was a misty image of Betsy twirling round the same hall before restoration had made the building habitable.

'Isn't it just amazing?' she had exclaimed in excited appeal on their very first visit to Lavender Hall, her face lit up like a Christmas tree.

'It needs to be demolished,' Nik had countered, unimpressed.

'It's not past saving,' Betsy had argued. 'Can't you feel the atmosphere? The character of the place?

Can't you imagine what it would look like with a little work?'

A little work with a wrecking ball, Nik had thought grimly, uninspired by the chipped and broken bricks and the floor puddled by drips from gaping windows and a leaking roof. She had dragged him off on a tour, chattering with bubbling enthusiasm about how the Elizabethan property was a treasure chest of history and on the endangered historic buildings list. Right from the start he had thought it was a horrible house and about as far removed from his idea of a comfortable and suitable country home as it was possible to imagine. But he had recognised that Betsy had fallen madly in love with the dump and, even though it wasn't what he wanted, he had agreed to buy it for her, a generous act that had rebounded on him many times in the following months when the costs of restoration had risen to outrageous levels.

Ne...yes, he *had* been a decent, caring husband, Nik reflected with brooding hostility. He had tried to make his wife happy, had given her everything she had ever wanted with the single exception of that last impossible demand of hers, and he still could barely credit that their marriage had been destroyed by her desire for, of all things, a baby. Her careless dismissal of the idea of having a child had been so convincing before their marriage.

Lean, strong face tensed by the forbidding tenor of his thoughts, Nik swung round with a frown just as Betsy surged through the kitchen door. She looked harassed, her pale blonde hair tumbling round her delicate, flushed features, making her eyes look more mauve in hue than ever and emphasising the pink, pillowy, luscious shape of her unpainted lips.

Instantaneous desire lit Nik up inside in a firework burst of startling heat that took his breath away. Without the smallest warning everything he had failed to feel in the limo with Jenna the day before surged through him, tightening every muscle in his body and setting off a fast-beating pulse at his groin that made him want to smash something in sheer frustration.

'Betsy,' he breathed in growling acknowledgement.

One glimpse of her visitor and Betsy had frozen in place like someone who had run head first into a solid brick wall. Why on earth hadn't Edna warned her? His sexy-as-sin voice washed over her like rich vanilla ice cream coated in melted dark chocolate, vibrating down her taut spinal cord… Nik's voice, the first weapon in his considerable arsenal of attraction. Nik here at the hall where she had never expected to see him again! His sudden appearance was a huge shock and she blinked rapidly and snatched in a stark breath, striving to brace herself for what could only be bad news of some kind.

'What are you doing here?' she gasped strickenly before she could think better of openly revealing her dismay.

'I needed to see you.'

Unconvinced, Betsy simply stared back at him. His dark grey pinstripe designer suit was faultlessly fitted to every muscular angle of his lean, powerful body. Big and strong, he was a brutal force of nature beneath that sleek, sophisticated façade he wore to the world. In all the months they had lived apart he had made not one single attempt to see her, so why now? Her brain, however, was stuttering to a halt when confronted with Nik in the flesh. Those lean, darkly beautiful features of his drew her in like a fire on a freezing day. She didn't want to look but she couldn't help herself. He had the gorgeous face and classic body of a mythical god, eyes shimmering bright as emeralds, awakening a primal attraction that was rooted so deep inside her she didn't know where it began or how she would ever be free of its sway. Her skin prickled, tiny hairs rising at the nape of her neck as she subdued a responsive shiver. Her heart was racing.

And then mercifully a voice from outside broke into the smouldering silence. 'Come back here!' a man was shouting.

The pitter-patter of rushing paws and an unforgettably familiar bark made Betsy's eyes fly wide in recognition and she hurtled to the door to peer out. An ecstatic bundle of wriggling, whining terrier dog leapt up into her arms and covered every part of her he could reach with delighted doggy kisses.

'I'm very sorry, sir. He leapt through the window of the car,' Nik's driver confided in breathless pursuit.

Nik was tempted to remark that that had to be the most life Gizmo had shown in the two months since he had retrieved the dog from Betsy. With a nod of dismissal to his driver, he thrust the front door closed with an impatient hand and studied the tableau before him. Betsy was down on her knees on the tiled floor smiling and laughing and the terrier was bouncing and leaping around her, the pair of them enacting a mutually jubilant reconciliation scene that even Nik could not remain untouched by. He knew he had made the right decision.

'You brought him here to visit me?' Betsy questioned, glancing up enquiringly, utterly confused by the dog's sudden appearance.

'No, he's here to stay,' Nik informed her wryly. 'He's not happy away from you.'

'But he's *your* dog,' she framed uncertainly, gathering Gizmo into her arms and stroking him to calm him down.

'He was only mine until he met you,' Nik retorted, compressing his mouth into a sardonic line while he noted as she bent over the dog the slight definitive bounce of her small breasts below her sweater, which told him that she was wearing nothing underneath. He became so hard in that split second that he was in literal pain.

Giving Gizmo back to her was an extraordinarily generous gesture and an astonishing move from a male as cold-blooded and unforgiving as Nik, Betsy reflected in bewilderment while she struggled to understand his reasoning. Unfortunately, Nik might be gorgeous but he was also complicated, impossibly so. She had never had much idea what went on inside his handsome head and once again he had taken her very much by surprise.

Gizmo was a stray, who had been knocked over by Nik's limousine months before Betsy even met Nik. He had taken the dog to a veterinary surgery for treatment and when nobody came forward to claim him he had asked the vet to try and find him a home. When that had failed, Nik had baulked at the prospect of putting the little dog into a council home for strays where he would ultimately be put down if he still failed to attract a new owner. Against all the odds, Nik had taken in Gizmo himself, introducing the little animal to a roof garden and a life of luxury food, dog walkers and groomers.

While Betsy reflected on Gizmo's humble beginnings as a stray, Nik was wishing he had stayed safe at the office. Watching Betsy shower affection on his dog filled him with conflicting feelings. He wanted to look at her but he didn't want to be with her or note the way the sunlight flooding through the windows gleamed over her impossibly pale blonde hair, accentuating her porcelain-perfect skin and haunting blue eyes. He especially didn't want the intensely sexual arousal currently coursing through his big, powerful body like a runaway train.

'Thank you from the bottom of my heart,' Betsy told him with tears in her eyes. 'I've missed him so much.'

Restored to his proper home, Gizmo trotted off cheerfully to explore his old haunts.

Nik studied Betsy with smouldering green eyes and her heart gave a sudden jarring thud.

Betsy *knew* that look of hunger on Nik's hard,

handsome face and it burned through her like a lightning strike, riveting her to the spot. That light in his stunning gaze told her that he wanted her and she couldn't stop her body reacting to that lure. An unbearable ache stirred at the apex of her slender thighs and she pressed them tightly together as if she could lock it in and deny it. Her breasts swelled beneath her sweater, making her all too aware of their bareness as her nipples were grazed by the wool.

'Come into the sitting room,' she urged, scrambling upright to lead the way as if he were a genuine guest visiting an unfamiliar place. 'Why didn't Edna tell me it was you?'

'I asked her not to. I wanted to surprise you.'

'Well, you've certainly done that,' Betsy admitted truthfully, struggling to credit that he was actually with her in what had once been the home they shared, even if it did cross her mind that Nik had spent more time in hotel rooms round the globe than he had ever spent with her. But that look he had given her—her thoughts raced back to that, worrying at it like a dog at a bone. *Why* had he looked at her like that? Surely he could not still find her attractive? Nik had been a less than enthusiastic lover in the last months of their marriage, although, now knowing about the vasectomy as she did, she could finally comprehend his loss of interest. Back then she had only thought of sex in terms of getting pregnant and she had no doubt that he had found her attitude a turn-off. No, don't think about sex, *don't think about sex,* she urged herself feverishly.

Betsy hovered awkwardly. 'Would you like a coffee?' she asked, because she was eager for the chance to escape to the kitchen for a few minutes and pull herself back together again.

'No, thanks, but I'll take a drink,' Nik declared, long, powerful legs carrying him across the room to the drinks cabinet, where he proceeded to help himself.

Unnerved by the fact that he could still confidently make himself at home while remaining utterly impervious to the discomfiture some men might have felt in the same situation, Betsy breathed in slow and deep to ground herself. 'I gather you want to talk—'

Nik spun back to her with the liquid grace of movement that always caught her eye and frowned at her, black brows drawing down, wide, sensual mouth twisting in dismissal. 'No. I don't want to talk,' he told her abruptly before he tossed back the finger of Scotch whisky he had poured neat and set down the empty glass again.

'Then…er…*why?*' she began in confusion.

His spectacular green eyes zeroed in on her with penetrating force and a flock of butterflies was unleashed in her tummy while her heartbeat kicked up pace again. 'I'm only here to return Gizmo.'

'Oh…' Betsy framed for want of anything better to say. A few months ago she would have shot accusations at him, demanded answers and would have thoroughly upset herself and him by resurrecting the past, which consumed her. But that time was gone, she acknowledged painfully, well aware that any reference to more personal issues would only send him out of the door faster. Nik had always avoided the personal, the private, the deeper, messier stuff that other people got swamped by. From the minute things went wrong in their marriage she had been on her own.

Nik scrutinised her lovely face, willing himself to find fault, urging himself to discover some imperfection that would switch his body back to safe neutral mode again. And yet on another level he was relieved, even satisfied by his arousal, grateful for the discovery that there was nothing at all amiss with his sex drive. Nor could he think of anything that could quench the swelling fullness of desire holding him rigid, unquestionably not the tantalising awareness that Betsy, all five feet nothing of her and regardless of her lack of experience before their marriage, was absolutely incredible in bed.

'*Se thelo*...I want you,' he heard himself admit before he was even aware that the words were on his tongue.

So Nik, *so* explosively unpredictable, Betsy reasoned abstractedly, colour rushing into her cheeks as a hot wave of awareness engulfed her. Jewel-bright eyes assailed hers in an almost physical collision and something low and intimate in her body clenched hard. Her legs turned so weak she wasn't convinced they were still there to hold her up but she was held in stasis by the intensity of his narrowed green gaze.

'And you want me,' he told her thickly. It was classic, pure textbook Nik to tell her what she was feeling before she even knew it herself.

And Betsy knew she ought to argue and defend herself while telling him all the many reasons why that could not possibly be true, not least the fact that his deception and his willingness to turn his back on their marriage had made her *hate* him with the same passion that she had once loved him.

But, inexplicably, in that rushing silence filled only with the accelerated thump of her heart in her own ears, she said nothing, couldn't find the words, indeed was plunged into so much confusion her mind was a mess of barely formed thoughts and reactions.

CHAPTER THREE

NIK STALKED FORWARD with slow predatory grace, yet
for all that there was barely a coherent thought in his
handsome dark head. There was no reason, only reaction, no motive other than a desire that gripped him
tighter than any vice, in fact a desire so powerful it
made him throb and ache.

He reached for Betsy, tugging her arms round his
neck, clamping her slim body close, sealing those
soft curves to his with a raw exhalation of relief he
could not suppress. Backing her to a wall, he raised
her high to seize her mouth and claim it, opening his
mouth over hers, using pressure to force an entrance
and then delving deep with a hungry, devouring passion that stole the breath from her lungs. He tasted of
whisky and spice and Betsy drank him in like an addictive drug, head spinning on an intoxicated high.
He kissed her as if his life and hers depended on it
and his raw urgency fired her up even more, her head
falling back to allow him greater access.

Betsy whimpered beneath his lips, holding herself
stiff while she fought a rearguard action in the back

of her mind in which a voice was screaming that she didn't want to do what she was doing. Unfortunately, she very much *did* want to do it at that moment when only passion ruled and reason couldn't get a look-in. She was no victim either. Her tongue tangled with his and teased back, her small hands kneading his strong arms, rejoicing in the strength of him but frustrated by the barrier of his clothing.

Nik curved his hands to her bottom below her skirt, discovering to his satisfaction that her love of skimpy underthings still reigned supreme, and with one violent wrench the lacy knickers were torn away. Betsy gasped in shock.

'You want me,' Nik husked in hoarse excuse against her swollen mouth, his warm breath fanning her skin.

Oh, *how* she had wanted, night after night, day after day, craving what she had lost, missing the passion and the closeness and the intimacy that had once been so much a part of her life while wondering if she would ever trust anyone enough to let them touch her again. Every screaming skin cell was conscious of the proximity of Nik's hand to the hottest, neediest place in her body and she couldn't vocalise, couldn't think of anything but the deep-down, all-encompassing hunger for his touch.

Bracing her to the wall, he thrust her sweater out of his path with an impatient hand to enable him to close his mouth hungrily round a plump pink nipple while his palm cupped the firm pouting curve. Betsy moaned, eyes tight shut, sensation darting down to the hot, liquid heart of her. A wild pulse of need was mounting there while he teased that tender swollen tip with the edges of his teeth and his tongue. Clinging to his shoulders, she spread her thighs and clamped them to his waist. Finally she could feel him even through his clothing, learn the hard, urgent thrust of his erection as he ground his hips into the apex of her slender thighs, provoking an impatient cry from her lips. Arching her pelvis into him, she shuddered and moaned.

They were acting like horny teenagers, she registered suddenly, in a short-lived burst of mental clarity and embarrassment. This is not me, this is *not* me. And it was her last chance to shout stop and her lips actually parted and then he found her with his hand, a long, knowing finger sliding into the hot, wet sheath of her body. In reaction, an explosion of fiery heat shot through her and she jerked against him, overwhelmingly eager for his touch, for anything that would assuage the intolerable scream of need building up so fast inside her that she could not contain it.

Nik struggled to support her at the same time as he unfastened his trousers. Betsy emitted a breathy moan when she felt him push against her. She was on a high of uncontrollable excitement, her hands biting into his shoulders, urging him on. He aligned their bodies, spreading her open before bringing her down on him. He sank into her slowly, stretching the sensitive tissue with his length and girth to the burning edge of pain. But it was so much a pleasurable pain that she almost wept at the thrill of his invasion because for the first time in many months she felt like a living, breathing woman again.

'Nik…?' she whispered shakily.

'No talk, *hara mou,*' he gritted, tilting her back at an angle, using the wall to partially support her as he slammed back into her again with sensual, dominant force. '*Thee mou,* what you do to me! Don't tell me to stop!'

At that moment Betsy wasn't capable of such a feat. She was already at fever pitch. An agony of desire and helpless need controlled her. Gripping her slender thighs, ebony-lashed green eyes blazing with emerald fire, Nik surged and retreated, keeping up the erotic pace with perfect timing. Her excitement rose with every driving thrust, pushing her higher and higher until finally she reached the crest and it shattered her, making her writhe and sob and cry out.

'That was spectacular…' Nik breathed raggedly as he lowered Betsy's legs slowly back to the floor. She was weak, dizzy, unsteady on her feet, and even he was trembling. What had he done? *Diavelos,* what had he done? Yet in spite of that rational voice inside his head, Nik shed his jacket, yanked free his tie, contriving both instinctive actions without once letting go of Betsy. He tugged her by the wrist across the floor to the rug by the dying fire and drew her down on it to face him on her knees. He laced both hands into her tumbled hair, palms framing her cheekbones, and kissed her again, sliding his tongue between her lips, skating it over the sensitive roof of her mouth until she quivered and her hands curved over his arms again to support herself.

She couldn't think, could barely breathe and could hardly believe that that single kiss had sent the heat surging again like a gushing river of liquid fire in her belly. Satiation was washed away by a renewed tingling and prickling of potent awareness that covered her entire skin surface with heat. He pulled her down, rearranging her legs to cradle him, pinning her beneath the weight and bulk of his lean, muscular body.

'I'm not done yet, *hara mou*,' he confessed thickly, luxuriant black lashes low over scorching emerald eyes, lean, strong face taut, cheekbones flushed.

Her hand rose of its own volition and she ran her fingertips along the mobile line of his often hard-set mouth. It had a softer, more flexible cast now. She thought of him bringing Gizmo home and she gazed up at him, curiously at peace with what had happened, her heart full to overflowing. After all, she never had been able to second-guess Nik's next move and she guessed she never would have that power because he was very much a law unto himself.

He shifted against her, lithe and dynamic as a jungle cat, and she felt him hard and ready again against her stomach. 'Don't ask me to stop,' he groaned.

'Take off your shirt,' she whispered, amazingly relaxed in his arms, marvelling at how right it felt to be there again although even in that instant, in a part of her brain, she wouldn't acknowledge she knew she would never be able to justify what she had done.

He levered back from her and hauled roughly at

the garment. A couple of buttons went flying and a long, brown, mouth-watering wedge of a six-pack male torso appeared between the parted edges. Her mouth ran dry, tiny little slivers of excitement sparking again. She arched up against him, revelling in the skin-to-skin contact she had never thought she would feel again with him. With a hungry sound in the back of his throat he kissed her again, sliding between her slender thighs, hitching her skirt with impatient hands.

'This time…*slow*,' he framed in raw promise.

'Am I the hare or the tortoise?' she teased.

'Something about you turns me into the hare every time.'

Betsy laughed. 'Is this us again?' she mumbled wonderingly.

'This is now, *only* now,' Nik contradicted with innate precision, covering her mouth again with his to silence her and stop the questions and then lingering to savour her.

He sank into her again as slowly as he had promised. The taste of him was still on her lips and she was achingly sensitive to his every movement. A long, breathy sigh was extracted from her.

'Too much?' he prompted, staring down at her.

'Not enough,' she said daringly. 'I'm not made of glass… I won't break!'

Her heart and her body jumped in concert when he twisted his lithe hips and added a more dominant flavour to his possession, sensation winging through her in slow, delicious waves. She closed her eyes to contain her feelings, the excitement catching at her again and flaring bright as a falling star, making every nerve ending strain in longing for the ultimate peak. He quickened his pace and delicious friction intensified the electrifying pleasure. She moaned and her voice rose against her volition into a cry of shocked release, her whole body shaking with the soul-deep force of it as he emitted a raw groan of pleasure.

Nik eased back from her, righting his clothing, reaching down to scoop her up into his arms.

'What are you doing?' she framed limply, eyes flying open.

'Taking you to bed, where we should have gone in the first place,' Nik informed her, striding across the hall towards the heavily carved staircase.

'What we did was more exciting,' Betsy mumbled, thinking of how very long it had been since they had done anything this instantaneous or uninhibited. For the first time she recognised how much her campaign to fall pregnant had cost them in terms of intimacy. Nothing had been the same once that process had started.

Nik carried her into the room they had once shared and froze by the side of the bed, scanning the unfamiliar surroundings. The décor had changed and even the furniture was new. His mouth quirked. The reality jolted him, pushing him in the direction of thoughts he was determined not to think just then. He settled her down on the wide, low bed and undressed her with cool efficiency, tugging off the sweater, unzipping her skirt and slipping off her shoes before pulling the duvet over her.

'I need a shower,' he admitted. 'Is there still one in the bathroom? Or have you got rid of that as well?'

Betsy almost laughed. 'Of course the shower's still in there.'

She lay watching him strip, a sight she had never thought to see again, and the experience felt utterly unreal. He strode naked into the bathroom, yet she had recognised his unease with his surroundings. He didn't like change; he never had. The new colour scheme and furniture had made him tense and uncomfortable. Well, what had he expected? That she would continue to live with the bed they had once shared, allowing her home to inflict constant wounding with memories of what they had once shared together and lost? No, at least Belle had helped Betsy to make that much of a fresh start.

Nik emerged from the bathroom still towelling dry his black hair. She was startled to notice that he was still fully aroused. Nik had assumed that Betsy would fall asleep, but she was awake, wide, evocative azure eyes pinned to him. She was snuggled down under the duvet, hair as pale as a young child's trailing across the pillow in tousled disarray. Would he simply have got dressed and left had she been conveniently asleep? He honestly didn't know the answer to that question. What he did know as he looked at her was that he wasn't yet ready to leave, and without hesitation he tossed back the duvet and climbed in beside her.

'It's the middle of the day,' she reminded him, colour heating her face.

'Are you only remembering that now?' Nik traded sardonically, and she might have snapped back had he not closed his arms round her and tugged her reassuringly close. 'What does it matter what time it is?'

'It doesn't,' she conceded and then said in a different tone altogether, *'Nik?'*

'Shush,' he breathed, fearful of what she might say, curving her up against his still taut and aroused length with an exhilarating sense of extraordinarily intense satisfaction.

'You're *still*—' she began.

'I am,' Nik agreed, draping her tiny body over top of him with care. 'Do you think you could do anything about that?'

'You're not joking, are you?' Betsy knew he wasn't joking because she could feel him hard as an iron bar beneath her.

'Evidently you make me insatiable, *hara mou*.'

Her palms curved to his broad shoulders. Nik had enormous reserves of charm when he chose to utilise them but it was a very long time since he had bothered to show her that side of him. As a result, the slashing charismatic smile that lit up his lean dark features literally mesmerised her, leaving her defenceless. He lifted his head and tasted her parted lips with an intensity that set up a chain reaction of response that slivered through her bloodstream and sprang a sneak attack on her. He tasted so good and his lean hands were stroking up and down her slender spine, finding spots that felt erogenous even though she knew they were not. Even sealed to the heat and hard muscularity of him, she shivered, her heart hammering again, astounded by events and yet covertly flattered by his unquenchable hunger for her.

'One more time and then you can sleep,' Nik husked, rolling her back against the pillows and leaning over her, his devastatingly dark and masculine attraction enhanced by the shadow of stubble beginning to roughen his lower cheekbones and jawline.

'Time off for good behaviour?' she teased.

Claiming her mouth hungrily again in answer, he caught a swollen nipple between finger and thumb and rubbed the tender tip. A flame darted anew through her slender length and centred at her core, renewing the throb of awareness she had believed quenched. 'You could always make me want you,' she breathed in a helpless admission.

'Once you only wanted me when it was the right day on your temperature chart,' Nik reminded her with more than a hint of ice in his dark deep voice.

Something shrivelled and died inside Betsy and she would have done anything not to have roused that memory, which tore an ugly hole in the cocoon of togetherness she had spun for them in her mind. She pressed up against him, flattening her breasts to his broad, hair-roughened chest, and nipped at his full lower lip in reproof. 'I don't have a chart any more—'

'*Siopi*...quiet,' he urged and kissed her until she couldn't remember what they had been talking about and, furthermore, no longer cared.

He tasted wonderful. He even smelled wonderful, the evocative scent that was uniquely him flaring her nostrils, firing her senses with a tormenting familiarity that made her feel ridiculously safe. Expert fingers traced her breasts and skimmed up the inside of her thigh, teasing, taunting until the torment made her squirm and twist and whimper in frustration, wanting, by then *needing* so much more. Only when the hunger he had skilfully awakened rose to an unbearable intensity did he shift over her, sliding into the honeyed welcome of her body with an ease and dexterity that made her cry out and arch her spine. And from that point on, once an answering passion had fully seized her, the tenor of his approach changed and his shallow thrusts became deep and strong and she could feel what control she retained slipping away as the excitement built and built until finally she came, screaming his name, and almost instantly fell into the deep sleep of complete exhaustion.

Darkness had fallen beyond the windows when a slight sound awakened Betsy. She lifted her head from the pillow and everything came flooding back with much the same effect as having a bucket of cold water thrown over her and she sat up with an abrupt start of energy. Nik was engaged in tying his tie in front of the cheval mirror in the corner and hot, mortified colour enveloped her from top to toe. She hugged the sheet, afraid to think, shrinking from the prospect of passing judgement on herself.

'You're leaving?' she whispered as she switched on the bedside lamp.

Nik swung round, eyes light and glittering in the shadows, reticence etched in every angle of his lean, strong face. 'I should've gone hours ago—'

'Were you planning to walk out without speaking to me first?' Betsy pressed tightly because her throat was closing over. She edged the sheet as high as she could, so tense that her muscles ached from the strain.

'That might have been easier for both of us,' Nik quipped, striding to the foot of the bed to gaze down at her from his considerable height.

'How so?'

'I've heard that *this*...' he shifted a fluid brown hand in a gesture that encompassed both her and the bed '...is quite common for couples going through a divorce.'

Betsy felt as if he had punched her in the stomach and she lost colour, her skin pulling taut across her fragile bone structure. 'Really?' she queried with no expression at all.

'Yes, really,' Nik fielded drily. 'It happens but it doesn't mean anything, doesn't change anything.'

For the very first time in her life, Betsy wanted another human being lying stone dead at her feet. But even then she wouldn't forgive Nik, she reckoned wildly, plunged as she was into an abyss of mortification and pain and, worst of all, the dreadful conviction that it was *her* mistake that had unleashed such a humiliation on her.

'Obviously, we're still getting a divorce,' Nik assured her, underlining the point quite unnecessarily as though he feared that she might be too stupid to get that message.

'Yes,' she agreed, knowing that even the sight of him falling down dead at her feet wouldn't satisfy her sufficiently. Hatred now leapt through her as fierily as the passion that had betrayed her. In spite of everything he had done to her, she had missed him, missed sex, and she was paying the price for her wretchedly poor judgement now.

'We both need to move on,' Nik breathed curtly.

'Until now I never appreciated what a taste you have for platitudes,' Betsy responded grittily. 'You have patronised me, insulted me and used me. Now I know what it feels like to be a booty call.'

Nik ground his teeth together. He had said what he had to say. He was exceptionally intelligent and he knew the score, even if calling it was insensitive. They had both made a mistake and it was his place to spell that out. He wasn't built to closely connect with another human being. After the abusive childhood he had endured, how could he possibly be? There was a lack in him, not in her, and he could never give her what she wanted and deserved.

'I'll let you keep the house as well,' he told her flatly.

'It's good to know I profited from prostituting myself,' Betsy hurled back at him shakily, tears burning the backs of her eyes like acid. 'For goodness' sake, *go!*'

And without fanfare that was exactly what Nik did. The door snapped shut in his wake but not before

Gizmo had inserted himself through the gap and hurtled towards his only recently rediscovered mistress.

'Oh, Gizmo…' she gasped, her voice catching on a sob as she hugged the shaggy little dog to her chest.

Nik had just walked out on her again. His driver would have sat outside waiting for him all these hours. That wouldn't bother Nik and he wouldn't apologise for his thoughtlessness either. The only child of a fabulously wealthy Greek heiress, Nik was accustomed to staff who never questioned or complained and he paid highly for a very high standard of service. A wife with a similar attitude would have suited him so much better than Betsy ever had. She had wanted too much from him and had fought her own corner too hard while demanding an independence of thought and action that had frequently infuriated him. But then bearing in mind his behaviour on their first catastrophic date, she really couldn't say that she hadn't been warned that nothing would be plain sailing with Nik Christakis at the helm…

And because the far distant past was less threatening than the turmoil of the present, she let her mind drift back to that evening and a wry smile formed on her lips. Nik had taken her to a glitzy party, where her little black dress unembellished by jewellery or a designer bag or shoes had failed to cut the mustard. Ten minutes after their arrival, Nik had excused himself and abandoned her, leaving her alone in a sea of strangers to be hit on by strange men and visually crucified by much-better-dressed women. After an hour and a half during which she had failed to find him she had angrily embarked on the long journey home by bus and train. He had turned up on her doorstep after midnight to furiously demand to know why she had walked out on him. And they had had their first row, a flaming no-holds-barred argument where he insisted he had only left her alone for about fifteen minutes.

'You were away well over an hour... You treated me like dirt. I should've known what kind of treatment I was in for when you picked me up and then spent the entire drive to the party talking to someone on your phone!'

He had forgotten the time; she knew that. It was also possible that he had even forgotten he had brought Betsy to the party in the first place because an old friend had offered him a deal and business always took precedence with Nik. He had sent her flowers every day for a week afterwards and had then visited the bistro for coffee every day the following week.

'You're acting like a stalker,' she had warned him.

'Give me one more chance. I'll treat you like a queen,' Nik had promised.

'You know, Mr Christakis doesn't usually go to so much trouble with women,' one of his bodyguards had told her chattily. 'You must be special.'

And when she had returned with Nik's coffee and those brilliant green eyes clung to her, she had realised that he did make her feel special. Everyone made mistakes, she had thought forgivingly; she would give him the chance to prove that he could act differently. And for a very long time afterwards she had not regretted that decision because Nik, she now recognised, had been on his very best behaviour. She even remembered the day he had asked her how she felt about having children. She couldn't remember how the dialogue had progressed in that direction but with hindsight suspected that he had guided it there.

'I don't want children!' she had proclaimed, wincing at the very idea. 'I spent my teenage years in foster homes and I spent a lot of time helping to look after the younger ones and the babies. Kids are so much work and such a tie. I don't think I'll ever want any.'

But Betsy had discovered the hard way that Mother Nature had amazing ways of working her wiles to persuade a woman that what she wanted most in the world was a little baby. When she'd first married Nik she had been Cinderella and he had been Prince Charming. He had given her so much in terms of material things that she had somehow never dared to complain that he was rarely at home and was invariably preoccupied with business even when he was. He had missed her birthday and their first anniversary and slowly but surely she had become incredibly lonely and had begun to crave what she had never dreamt she would crave—a baby to love and keep her company.

In the grip of that desire she had made stupid optimistic assumptions, believing that Nik would spend more time at home if they had a child, that a child to share would bring them closer, hopefully breaking through his reserve as she had already discovered she could not.

She had made so many mistakes with Nik, Betsy acknowledged wretchedly, dabbing her damp cheeks dry on the sheet, soothing Gizmo when he whined and pushed his muzzle under her hand. But Nik had made just as many mistakes with her. Getting back into bed with him again, however, had to qualify as her crowning act of stupidity. Her face burned hot while her body ached in silent evidence of her weakness. Afterwards, Nik had been so cold, so sure that their renewed intimacy meant nothing. Why? Because it had meant nothing to him and he had been appalled by the idea that she might think otherwise.

Once again, Nik had taught her a hard lesson. A woman worthy of being treated like a queen had to maintain standards to exercise that power over a man. When she abandoned those standards, she was infinitely more likely to be treated like a booty call.

CHAPTER FOUR

'BETSY?' CRISTO'S WIFE, Belle, questioned eagerly.
'Why haven't you been answering your phone? Where
have you been? What have you been up to?'

It was a bad moment for her friend to have phoned
because Betsy couldn't concentrate. Betsy sank weakly
down on an armchair and contemplated the results
of her insane shopping trip to the nearest pharmacy:
no less than *five* separate pregnancy-testing kits. And
each and every one of the kits had given her the same
answer. Ironically she was deeply familiar with such
testing procedures. When she and Nik had still been
together, whenever her menstrual cycle had shown the
slightest deviation, she had rushed out to buy a test,
inwardly praying for a positive result and each and
every time she had been disappointed it had broken
her heart afresh.

This time around, however, everything was very
different. Betsy had been feeling out of sorts for
weeks before she finally went to visit her GP and
she had gone there without the smallest suspicion of
the truth now facing her. Indeed she didn't know how

she would ever walk through the door of the doctor's surgery again without feeling embarrassed. A simple test had disclosed the fact that she had inexplicably conceived and her response to the news had been more than a little hysterical while she told first the doctor and then the nurse that there had been a mistake, that they must have mixed up her results with someone else's and that in any case, a pregnancy was a complete impossibility.

'*Betsy?*' Belle exclaimed. 'Are you still there?'

'Yes, sorry, I'm just a little preoccupied right now.'

'It's the divorce, isn't it?' her friend said grimly. 'You've been upset. That's why you haven't been in touch. What has that wretched man done to you now?'

Betsy compressed her lips, because astonishingly it seemed that Nik *had* contrived the impossible. In spite of the fact that he'd had a vasectomy and he was sterile, or whatever people chose to label it, and she had endured many months of striving to get pregnant by him and failing, a miracle or a catastrophe—depending on one's viewpoint—had occurred and she was now carrying Nik's baby. How on earth *could* that be possible? Betsy breathed in deep and slow because even sitting down she felt giddy and more than a little nauseous.

'It's not something I can share,' Betsy said, inwardly wincing at that severe understatement.

'Something happened when Nik brought Gizmo back to you…didn't it?' Belle prompted worriedly. 'You haven't been yourself since then—'

'Yes, something happened,' Betsy confirmed

reluctantly. 'But not something I can talk about right now—'

The pregnancy that she had once craved had actually materialised but she no longer had the support system of either a marriage or a father for her unborn child. That awareness put a very different complexion on the situation.

'I just knew it was too good to be true when he gave you the dog back!' Belle exclaimed heatedly. 'And then the house, for goodness' sake! Nik Christakis suddenly starts playing Santa Claus! There's something wrong with that image—'

'I promise I'll phone you in a few days when I've sorted stuff out,' Betsy cut in ruefully. 'I'm sorry but I just can't talk about this yet.'

Betsy switched off her phone and stared into space, rather than at the testing kits and packaging. There was no avoiding her next step: she needed Nik to explain how she could have fallen pregnant by a man who'd had a vasectomy. She could not possibly keep her condition a secret from him. Nik had to be told that he was going to be a father, whether he liked the idea or not. No, without a doubt, Nik had to be informed that he had got her pregnant and he had to be forced to accept that fact even if it meant the humiliation of having to undergo DNA testing as evidence after their child was born. Betsy was already excruciatingly aware that Nik would not want their child and would probably much prefer to believe that she had fallen pregnant by some other man, thereby absolving him from all responsibility and the threat of a continuing connection to the wife he could hardly wait to divorce.

Over the past two months Betsy's spirits had steadily sunk into the doldrums. Coming to terms with the explosive passion that had plunged her into renewed sexual intimacy with her estranged husband had proved a mammoth challenge. The emotional wound Nik had inflicted was almost as great as the agony of feeling that she had seriously let herself down. Yet she wasn't a victim, wasn't a weakling, wasn't one of those women who forgave a man no matter how badly he treated her. She had *not* forgiven Nik and she was mortified that she had gone to bed with him again.

What had made her feel even worse was the painfully obvious fact that Nik could not wait to draw a double black line below their marriage and mark it finished. He had returned Gizmo, and just two weeks earlier had offered her a very generous final financial settlement through his lawyers. All the writing was on the wall. He wanted out of their marriage fast. She knew how Nik operated. He was stubborn and impatient and as cutting as a polished steel blade. He didn't waste time with anything he didn't want, and anything he did want he wanted it yesterday and he most definitely *wanted* the divorce.

So, how was she to approach a male so eager to cut their final ties and forget about her and tell him news that he couldn't possibly want to hear? Her small shoulders straightened with sudden spirit and purpose. Well, tough for Nik! He had got her pregnant, hadn't he? He was the one who had neither warned her of that risk nor guarded her against it and the consequences were as much his fault as her own. He might not want children but the warmth stealing through Betsy at the knowledge that she carried her first child was already infiltrating the shock value of the same discovery. She wanted *her* baby and she knew he would not. The facts were there. A male who had had a vasectomy at such a young age could *never* have wanted a child. But mercifully what Nik wanted no longer needed to influence her, Betsy acknowledged with relief, and allowing herself to be intimidated by a development for which they were both equally responsible would be silly and spineless, and Betsy was neither of these things.

'It's not convenient. Inform her that I will be in touch.' With difficulty Nik swallowed his ire at the polite lie he was being forced to utter before setting his phone down and returning to his business meeting.

Evidently Betsy had shown up uninvited and was waiting outside his office to see him. What on earth had come over her? She was well aware that he hated being interrupted for any reason during working hours. His perfect white teeth gritted, anger at her lack of consideration stirring. If she had something she needed to say to him she had a lawyer to act as her spokesperson, as did he. He did not want personal contact with her; he wanted a smooth, clean and civilised divorce.

Even so, a defiant image glimmered in the back of

his mind, a frankly licentious image of Betsy's slender, perfect body splayed across that bed at Lavender Hall, and outraged by that unwelcome intrusion, he kicked the image out again, wide, sensual mouth settling into a tense line of compression. Sleeping with Betsy again had been like turning over a stone, because all sorts of things he would rather not deal with had come tumbling out in the aftermath. Given time, however, the memories would fade and disappear, he assured himself resolutely.

He had paid absolutely no heed to his therapist's suggestion that he was deeply conflicted on the subject of his marriage. In that line the lady talked a lot of nonsense! Nik believed in keeping things simple and he fully understood why he had done what he had done. He had gone off the rails and fallen back into a better-forgotten past for a few hours…that was *all*. Soon his marriage would be as decently buried as the terrifying nightmares and flashbacks that had plagued him for years already were.

Betsy listened with a polite smile to the message Nik's stalwart PA, Steve, passed on with fervent apologies that she was persuaded had not fallen from Nik's lips. But Steve, unlike his boss, was a nice guy. Once upon a time Betsy's very rare visits to Nik's office building had been greeted with disconcerting attention and servility because she had been deemed a person of importance in Nik's world. Now, however, it was clear that she had lost that polished passport to special treatment and was viewed as being about as relevant to Nik as yesterday's newspaper.

'Thanks, Steve,' she said, sweeping up her sensible leather rucksack bag, ruefully conscious that her casual jeans and plain black pea coat had attracted raised brows of surprise since her arrival.

But then probably for the very first time ever, Betsy was happy to simply be herself in Nik's sophisticated radius, not the more glossy, artificial self she had long believed he found infinitely more attractive. So, she hadn't dressed up for his benefit and wasn't wearing high heels, designer clothing or even very much make-up. Nik was the husband who had deceived her, hurt her and humiliated her and she was determined to seek neither his approval nor his admiration.

As the PA walked away Betsy moved purposely in the opposite direction to head straight for Nik's office. Nik had wasted enough of her morning and she wasn't prepared to kick her heels any longer on his behalf! Why should she? She was no longer eager to please and conform to nonsensical rules that had once made her feel more like an irrelevant nuisance than a legally wedded wife with rights and needs of her own.

Betsy thrust Nik's office door wide, scanning the half-dozen men seated round the small conference table with flaring midnight-blue eyes of enquiry before settling her attention on Nik's lean, hard-boned face. 'I need to see you...*now,*' she declared without hesitation.

A feverish glimmer of dark colour rose to accentuate the exotic line of Nik's hard cheekbones, his green eyes flaring like emeralds in bright sunlight to betray more than a glint of outrage. He stood upright, lithe and fit as the predator he was, and shifted a hand in dismissal as Steve raced through the door a mere breathless step in Betsy's wake.

'Gentlemen, we'll have to take a break. I'll see you in an hour,' Nik informed his companions flatly.

The other men filed out and the door snapped shut behind Betsy. Her attention had not once wavered from Nik. Even his business suit couldn't hide the lean, powerful perfection of his athletic body. She remembered the appalling nightmares he used to have and how even though it was the middle of the night he would go down to the basement gym to work out afterwards, before finally falling back exhausted into bed still wet from the shower.

Immobile as a statue now, she could hear her own breath scissoring audibly through her tight throat while her heart thumped so hard with stress she would have liked to press a hand to her chest to slow it down. But that, much like apologising, would have been a dead giveaway of her inner turmoil and Betsy had no intention of making such a crucial error in Nik's forceful and assured presence.

'What the hell are you playing at?' Nik demanded in a harsh undertone, appraising her unfamiliar appearance with a frown of incomprehension.

For some inexplicable reason she was dressed like a student and she looked impossibly young, blue eyes huge in her delicate heart-shaped face. She was five years younger than him, *only* five and yet sometimes the distance between them had seemed an unbridgeable gulf because she had a quality of innocence and a level of trust in other people that he had lost at a very early age. But then if he was honest that difference in their outlook had been a strong part of her appeal, he acknowledged reluctantly. He had known she would always need his strength to protect her while also knowing that love made her loyal and naively trusting and that she would always be there waiting for him in the background.

And even with her dressed as carelessly as she was now, Betsy's beauty still rocked him where he stood. That awareness shook him because it seemed as though all his mental prompts that she was imperfect had only highlighted the fact that she somehow made imperfection the absolute definition of pure exquisiteness on his terms. Instinctive desire kindled in him, his temperature rising, his libido purring into gear. His keen gaze lingered on the lush curve of her mouth and the tender white of her fragile throat where it emerged from a roll-neck sweater while he remembered the taste of her mouth and the feel of it on him.

'It's payback time…the magic moment when all your sins come home to roost,' Betsy told him in direct challenge, absolutely determined not to be apologetic or, indeed, understanding of the mistake he had made. 'And you have to explain something to me. You had a vasectomy, so how the heck did you get me pregnant?'

Disconcerted by that highly provocative opening assault, Nik froze to the carpet in front of her, sleek ebony brows rising, nostrils flaring. Betsy worked really hard at not noticing his glossy gorgeousness. But memory was flashing debilitating images through her brain: her fingers sliding through the shiny black silk of his hair, her thumb smoothing the sexy line of that full, wonderfully sensual lower lip. With great difficulty she suppressed her wandering thoughts.

'*Pregnant?*' Nik repeated that word in outright disbelief. 'What are you talking about?'

Betsy recognised that she still had the advantage because she had taken him totally by surprise. 'I'm pregnant and I haven't been with anyone but you,' she informed him bluntly. 'So explain to me how that is possible.'

For the first time in his life, Nik was speechless. *Pregnant?* All his natural colour drained from beneath his bronzed skin as he took a sudden step back from her, stunned eyes locked to her in unconcealed shock while a shard of bone-deep fear sliced unequivocally through his big frame. 'You're…pregnant?' he breathed in a roughened undertone, his scepticism concerning her claim blatant.

'*Explain* that to me,' Betsy urged impatiently.

Nik raked long brown fingers through his blue-black hair, a dazed aspect to his usually shrewd gaze as he stared steadily back at her. 'You've found out that you're pregnant? *Seriously?*'

'Do I look like I'm joking?' Betsy shot back at him defensively.

A deep frown line pleated Nik's brows and there was a pause before he spoke again because his brain refused to accept what she had just told him. 'I had the vasectomy reversed,' he admitted without any expression at all.

Betsy took a sudden step forward, moving closer to him without even being aware of the movement. 'Reversed…*when?*' she queried, suddenly desperate to hear that answer.

'After you threw me out—'

'But…*why?*' she prompted, wondering if he had hoped to get her back with that news and if so why he hadn't approached her at the time.

'I realised it was time that I trusted myself to be in charge of my own fertility. I didn't even know the vasectomy *could* be reversed when we broke up. I always assumed it was final,' he admitted curtly, speaking with a candour she was unaccustomed to him using. 'When I found out that a reversal may well be successful if done within ten years of the original op, I decided to go for it. I was supposed to return for tests after the procedure to see if it had worked but I'm afraid I was so busy I never got around to it…'

Betsy's lashes wavered slowly up and down as she tried to process that unexpectedly detailed reply. But no matter how often she thought that response over she couldn't make sense of it. What did he mean about trusting himself to be in charge of his own fertility? What on earth was he talking about? And why the heck would he have had the procedure reversed *after* they had separated and not even bother to tell her about it? Well, that was one question answered loud and clear, she acknowledged painfully. Evidently his decision to have his vasectomy reversed had had nothing whatsoever to do with either her or her longing for a baby or the saving of their marriage. It was yet another slap in the face for Betsy, another wounding reminder that she never had understood and never would understand what made Nik Christakis tick.

'You are honestly pregnant?' Nik pressed her, studying her with frowning intensity and a lingering sense of disbelief because that possibility still didn't feel real to him. He might now have the proof that the reversal had worked but he was equally appalled by the risk he had unwittingly run and the unthinkable consequences of his evidently restored fertility. This result was his fault, solely *his* fault for neglecting to recall the fact that for the first time ever with Betsy he would need to take precautions.

Diavelos, suppose he *had* slept with another woman? Suppose he had been having this exact same conversation with a woman who was almost a stranger? But then would he have been so careless with anyone other than Betsy? He didn't think so. Once again familiarity had worked against him with Betsy, but then it had been so many years since he had had to guard against the risk of an unwanted pregnancy that he had behaved as imprudently as a teenager eager to have sex for the first time at any cost.

'One hundred per cent pregnant,' Betsy extended curtly, whipping her attention off his lean, darkly beautiful face when she felt it wanting to loiter, stifling her reaction to him with every fibre of her self-discipline because it was screamingly inappropriate. For the sake of the future and her unborn child she had to stick to cold, hard facts. 'So you accept that you're to blame for this pregnancy and that this will be *your* child?'

Lush spiky black lashes narrowed over suddenly astute green eyes, bright chips of colour in his lean, strong face. 'Have you any doubt on that score?' he questioned drily.

Betsy lifted her chin, azure eyes full of scornful dismissal. 'None at all.'

'Are you pleased?' Nik asked her without warning because he literally couldn't think of anything else to say and was wary of saying the wrong thing. A baby. Betsy was having a baby, *his* baby. Her announcement had plunged him deep into shock. He couldn't compute a concept so foreign to him for he had never once actively considered becoming a father. Reversing the vasectomy had been much more of an intellectual and philosophical exercise than an actual wish to see a child of his own blood born. Indeed that was a development that even at his most optimistic he had never once dared to envisage. After all, children were so vulnerable and no matter how hard one might endeavour to protect a child bad things still happened to them. At the thought, Nik paled.

Betsy breathed in so deep and long that she felt giddy. 'Am I *pleased?*' she repeated in charged disbelief, her small body turning rigid with the force of her feelings. 'Are you kidding? I wanted a baby when we were married. I wanted a family. *This...*' she spread her arms wide in emphasis, as if encompassing the distance now between them '...is not what I wanted!'

'So you don't want the baby,' Nik assumed, wondering how he felt about that but still too shaken by her news to know. A baby. Betsy was going to have a baby, the first Christakis infant to be born since his own birth.

'It's my baby...*of course* I want it!' Betsy slung back at him with an aggression she had never shown him before, no, not even on the day their marriage had tumbled down like a pack of cards and she had virtually thrown him out of their home. 'You need to know now upfront that there's no way I'm having a termination—'

'I am not that stupid,' Nik fielded flatly. 'Nor would I ask you to do such a thing.'

'*No?*' Betsy's voice was steadily rising in volume even though she was struggling to stay calm, well aware that a loss of temper was a handicap she didn't need. 'Wouldn't you? Wouldn't a termination suit you much better than the birth of a child you don't want?'

'Don't put words in my mouth. I didn't say I didn't want the child,' Nik countered darkly. 'Obviously, you do—'

Betsy was in no mood to allow him to make assumptions and she was frustrated by his failure to give her a single hint of his true feelings. 'Why? What's obvious about it? Because you're wrong—everything's changed. I never wanted to be a single parent raising a child alone!'

Nik clenched his teeth together on an ill-considered retort. She was pregnant. Betsy was pregnant, he reflected abstractedly, marvelling at the development that had come too late to save them. Whether she would admit it or otherwise, he had finally contrived to give her the one thing she truly wanted and he was violently disconcerted by the flare of satisfaction that infiltrated him at that acknowledgement. He didn't want to think about the baby; he wanted to think about what the baby would mean to *her,* and he was convinced that that child would mean the world to Betsy.

He remembered the secret stash of baby clothes he had stumbled on in the back of the closet and the sickening sensation of futility and powerlessness that had engulfed him that evening. He couldn't tell her the truth about his past; he could *never* tell her the truth, for how would she regard him afterwards? He had only had his pride left to sustain him. He had known from the outset that silence was his only possible defence, but her announcement had engulfed him like a hurricane, throwing into chaos everything he had believed he felt and thought.

'*You* made it that way for me!' Betsy continued in angry condemnation. 'You didn't give me a choice. You didn't warn me I *could* get pregnant—'

Nik released his breath in an impatient sound and replied with innate practicality, 'I don't think contraception was uppermost in either of our minds that day. I didn't think about anything that prosaic—'

'Oh, I can believe *that* all right!' Betsy flamed back at him, eyes hurling furious derision, ripe mouth curved with unfamiliar scorn. 'All you were thinking about was sex!'

'Be practical…what else would I be thinking

about?' Nik traded evenly, not one whit perturbed by that indictment. 'You didn't hold back either.'

Betsy wanted to slap him for that insolent reminder. Had she behaved like a sensible, self-respecting woman, nothing would've happened. She would have looked at him in shock and said no straight away when he came on to her. But she had never found it possible to look at Nik and say no and that went right to the heart of their relationship. The balance of power in the sex department had always been his until she had thrown a spanner into the works by craving a child and a whole new schedule during which Nik's desire for her had noticeably declined. Colour infusing her cheeks, she studied his desk. 'I totally hate and despise you—'

'We must be practical,' Nik murmured softly, much as if she hadn't spoken. 'Drama and accusations of blame will get us nowhere—'

'That's very easy to say from where you're standing,' Betsy riposted bitterly. 'Your whole life isn't going to be disrupted by single parenthood!'

'Both our lives will be disrupted,' Nik countered drily. 'But as lack of resources is not a problem I believe we will survive the challenge. I will naturally ensure that you have all the support you require from this point on—'

People he would pay to take the physical work and round-the-clock responsibility out of parenting, Betsy interpreted in even greater disgust. He wasn't volunteering himself; he wasn't willing to make a single sacrifice. And why would he be when he didn't want to be a father in the first place? she asked herself painfully.

'Stuff your blasted resources!' Betsy slung at him, vitriolic in the grip of her resentment, her heart-shaped face flushed with fury, eyes hurling don't-give-a-damn defiance. 'All I ever wanted was a *father* for my baby, not access to your wallet!'

Nik settled lacerating sea-green eyes on her, derision shimmering in every angle of his lean dark features. 'Am I supposed to be impressed by that statement? Until very recently you were claiming half of everything I own,' he reminded her with razor-edged cool.

Betsy squared her slim shoulders and hitched her bag, determined not to show weakness. 'And instead I've done even better,' she quipped. 'A baby has to be a virtual lifelong meal ticket!'

Nik surveyed her with chilling detachment. 'Go home, Betsy, before I lose my temper,' he urged.

And Betsy couldn't get out of his office fast enough and didn't breathe again until she was safe in the lift, whirring back down to the ground floor. Playing up to his view of her as a gold-digger might momentarily have seemed a way to save face, but in the long term it was a very bad idea, she reflected shamefacedly, particularly if it soured relations between them even more. What happened to her brain around Nik? She had just called her baby a lifelong meal ticket and she cringed at the awareness, knowing that even screaming abuse at Nik would have been preferable to the not so subtle weapon she had employed to fight her own corner.

And why had she behaved that way? She hated the way he had made her feel, hated that a moment that should have been exceptional and a cause for celebration had been destroyed by his shocked recoil in the face of her news. But then why was she still looking for the kind of response from Nik that he could never give her? He didn't want a child and she was having a child. Being disappointed wasn't an option, she told herself angrily. It was time to grow up and accept her world as it was, not as she would like it to be. In any case, hadn't Nik reacted better than she had hoped? There had been no demand for DNA testing, no suggestion that he suspected she might have fallen pregnant by another man.

Emerging into the fresh air, Betsy glanced across the street to where the bistro in which she had once worked had long since been replaced by an upmarket estate agency. Her troubled face tensed and then softened when she allowed herself to remember that, with savage irony, Nik Christakis had truly treated her like a queen *before* their marriage.

Sadly, Betsy had fallen in love with Nik so fast and so terrifyingly deeply that she had lost herself in him. When he had been with her he had become all that mattered and when he had been abroad he had been all she could think about and she had been wretchedly unhappy without him. Until she had met Nik she had not even known that she *could* feel such powerful emotion. She had begun skipping her night classes when Nik had wanted to see her and soon she had fallen behind with her assignments and stopped attending altogether. She was still ashamed of that short-sighted loss of drive back then and the inherent weakness of dropping her life plan in favour of a man and a relationship that might not have lasted. She had never dreamt that she was that kind of woman, but loving Nik had humbled her.

When Nik had asked her to marry him, she had been stunned, for she'd had no idea that he was that serious about her. At that point she hadn't even slept with him and his restraint in that department had already surprised her.

'You're a virgin, aren't you?' he had prompted after dinner in a trendy restaurant one evening. 'I don't mind waiting until you feel ready to share my bed. In fact the very act of waiting is refreshing and remarkably exciting.'

They had married in a welter of orange blossoms and flash photography, surrounded by hundreds of guests she hadn't known and only a handful that she had. Within weeks of the wedding, however, Nik had begun to change and recently she had wondered if he had changed towards her for the most demeaning reason of all. With the exciting chase ending on their wedding night when he finally got her into bed, had her driven alpha-male husband then begun to steadily lose interest because he was bored with her? After all, an inexpert non-virgin had little in the way of novelty to offer a sexual sophisticate.

But Betsy had predictably hung on in there, struggling to make a success of a marriage with a constantly absent partner. She had foolishly believed that a baby would bring them closer together and break through Nik's increasing detachment and reserve. And then one evening when Nik was abroad on business she had attended a dinner party at Cristo's, where Zarif, Nik's royal kid brother, had made an effort to chat to her and get to know her. When he had asked her how she managed when Nik was out of the country so often, she had briefly mentioned that now that the work on Lavender Hall was complete she was hoping to start a family soon, and Zarif had given her a startled look and asked how she planned to achieve that when Nik had had a vasectomy. That bombshell had come at her out of nowhere and within days had blown their marriage sky-high.

Now the world seemed to have turned full circle, Betsy acknowledged forlornly. She was getting the baby she had once craved but she no longer had a husband or a man willing to play the role of father. Their marriage was over even though the divorce had yet to be finalised.

CHAPTER FIVE

NIK WAS HAVING a very bad day. It had crashed and burned the minute Betsy had given him her news and he had found it impossible to concentrate after her departure. Having cancelled his meetings and told his PA to hold his calls, Nik walked out onto the roof garden of his apartment. He was home in the middle of the day and not working and it felt seriously strange. It was quiet and there was not even a breath of a breeze and only the dulled roar of the traffic far below. He would never have admitted it but he missed Gizmo, who had at least been company of a sort.

In the past, Nik had been a serious loner until he'd met Cristo and somehow contrived to bond with his brother in spite of the fact that they were very different men. Now he stared out unseeingly at the skyline and the rooftops. He led an immensely privileged existence and nobody needed to remind him of that fact. In almost every corner of his life his great wealth had smoothed his progress and thrust him onward and upward. But in one department his billions had always failed him and that was in the sphere of personal happiness.

It was possible though, he conceded broodingly, that he just didn't have what it took to experience joy. A lifetime of repressing his emotions and keeping secrets had damaged him, not to mention his ability to trust and sustain relationships. He had fought that truth for a long time and only recently come to accept that it was an inescapable fact.

Just as his dark and dreadful background was inescapable, he acknowledged grimly, Betsy's announcement along with her condemnation had unleashed some seriously unwelcome memories. Just at that moment he was recalling his first day at school, or, more accurately, the nightmare journey there in a chauffeur-driven car with a mother who had an uncontrollable temper.

'Having you has totally wrecked my life!' Helena had screamed at him resentfully, her clenched fist flying out to catch him a stinging blow across the cheek because she was enraged that his grandfather had insisted she get out of bed to accompany her four-year-old son. 'You ruined my body, you ruined my social life, you're preventing me from travelling or doing *anything* I enjoy… What else are you going to ruin, you little freak?'

Helena Christakis had never wanted to *be* a mother but when her deeply conservative father threatened to disinherit her after she conceived a child with her latest lover, Gaetano Ravelli, Helena had been forced for the first time in her self-indulgent life to deal with penalties. Faking a marriage to Gaetano to satisfy her father had been the first consequence and one that had ultimately paid off in terms of conserving her fortune. Unfortunately the ongoing responsibility of a child and the curtailment of Helena's freedom to do exactly as she liked had been a much more onerous punishment.

Not for one moment did Nik credit that Betsy could ever be as cruel, selfish or violent as his own mother had been throughout his childhood. He couldn't believe she would ever hate her child as his mother had often hated him while blaming him for every disappointment in her life. Even so, Nik could certainly accept that Betsy had conceived their child in far less rosy circumstances than those that she had originally foreseen. *Their* child? Even inside his head that label felt unnatural, unreal because he could not even begin to imagine the reality of such a development, for he had never had the smallest thing to do with pregnant women or children.

But what was done was done and Nik had always been a pragmatist. He had no doubt that if he failed to step up to the plate some other man would replace him as both husband to Betsy and father figure in their child's life. And that development would be totally unacceptable to Nik. There could be no halfway measures, he conceded broodingly. Either he became fully involved in his child's life or he would find himself excluded because a young and rich divorcee with Betsy's looks would not remain single for long. Yet how *could* he embrace everything that he had *always* avoided and feared? Fatherhood, with all the concerns and dangers that came with the responsibility. He breathed in slow and deep, eyes bleak, wide, sensual mouth clenching hard with constraint. He would do it the same way he had survived his brutal childhood: by never looking back to relive a better-forgotten past and taking only one step forward at a time.

'So, *spill,*' Belle urged. A tall, vibrant redhead, she threw herself back into the comfortable embrace of a purple velvet sofa and regarded Betsy with unconcealed expectancy in her lively eyes.

'I'm pregnant,' Betsy blurted out, having come to visit to make exactly that announcement.

Perceptibly disconcerted, her sister-in-law sat forward in a sudden movement. 'How the heck did you sneak having a man in your life past my radar?' she demanded in disbelief.

'Because he was already there…well, sort of,' Betsy muttered ruefully. 'It's Nik's baby—'

'Nik? How *could* it be Nik's?'

'You must not mention this to Cristo yet. It's private…between Nik and me,' Betsy extended awkwardly, wishing that Cristo's wife would stop studying her as though she were waiting for the clowns to come trooping in and provide a comic act. In as few words as she could manage she revealed that Nik had had the vasectomy reversed.

Belle blinked slowly. 'OK,' she conceded. 'And then he gave you the dog back and clearly you slept with him out of gratitude—'

'It wasn't like that,' Betsy countered quietly.

'I know you. You're very soft-hearted. He took advantage—'

'Maybe I took advantage of him...'

Belle was shaking her head in wonderment. 'Wow...just wow. Nik's going to be a dad. Considering that he can't even bear to be in the same room with my siblings that scenario takes quite a stretch of the imagination—'

Betsy was fond of Cristo's wife but had never appreciated her outspokenly critical attitude towards Nik. 'You're not being fair, Belle. Nik never knew his own father and has never had anything to do with children. Gaetano Ravelli walked out of his life when he was a baby and Nik never saw him again, so it's a lot harder for him to feel that there's a family connection with the younger brothers and sisters that you and Cristo have adopted.'

Franco, the youngest of those children, an adorable toddler with curly black hair and big brown eyes, clambered onto his half-sister Belle's lap and hugged her with easy affection. It was clear that he regarded Belle very much as his mother, yet Franco and his four siblings were actually the progeny of Belle's late mother's long-running affair with Nik and Cristo's now-deceased father.

For the first time though, Betsy was also registering an odd fact that made her brow furrow in surprise. Almost *everything* she knew about Nik's family background had come from either Cristo or Belle because Nik never ever talked about his childhood. His relationship with his mother was quietly dysfunctional and something he politely refused to discuss.

Betsy had only met Helena Christakis once when the older woman had evidently surprised Nik by choosing to attend their wedding. Helena had arrived with her latest boyfriend in tow and had avoided all but the most fleeting contact with her son and his bride. Even so, Helena's presence must've proved more of a punishment than a pleasure for her son because she had worn a dress more suited to a teenager, had got distinctly drunk and at one stage had chosen to recline on her toy boy's lap and behave like a sex kitten. Nik had seemed impervious to his mother's behaviour and had made no comment. At the time Betsy had naively assumed that he was hiding his embarrassment but she had since learned to appreciate that virtually nothing embarrassed Nik.

'It was a challenge for Cristo as well,' the other woman reasoned. 'He wasn't into kids either but I don't think he was ever as set against the idea of them as Nik has always seemed to be. When do you plan to tell him about the baby?'

'I've already told him… This morning, in fact. That's why I came up to London.' Betsy compressed her lips because she had no intention of sharing any further information, but then she could scarcely have hoped to conceal a pregnancy from close friends and family. And more than anything else that was what Cristo and Belle had become to Betsy—family, the family she'd never really had. They had both made time in their busy lives for her during the gloomy, heartbreaking months of her marriage breakdown, always ready to listen and support and offer soothing words.

'And?'

'Well, at least Nik didn't suggest that the baby might be some other man's—'

'Why would he when you've been living like you've taken a vow of celibacy?' Belle demanded with a wry roll of her eyes. 'A child is going to make everything so much more difficult and complicated for you.'

'I don't see why,' Betsy replied in a fiercely upbeat tone as she tilted her chin. 'I have a business, a home and a devoted dog. The baby will slot right in there perfectly and life will go on.'

Soon after that, Betsy got up to leave because the emotional turbulence of her day had exhausted her and she was looking forward to getting home and relaxing in front of the fire with Gizmo as a foot warmer. Belle pulled open the drawing room door for her. 'Oh, before I forget, you're booked to come to my birthday party a week on Friday. I've even arranged a lift for you—'

'A…lift?' Betsy repeated in surprise.

'Chris Morrison. He lives by you and he said he'd be happy to bring you with him, so you won't even have to stay the night here because he'll take you home again as well,' Belle revealed with satisfaction. 'I passed on your number so that he can contact you to arrange a time.'

'Who is he?' Betsy prompted with a frown, recognising how Belle had cleverly boxed her in and made it impossible for her to refuse to attend. Her momentary spark of resentment at being managed, however, evaporated when she pictured herself sitting home alone every night moping. Nik wasn't moping; no, her soon-to-be ex was regularly linked to society beauties, whom he escorted to clubs, art galleries and opera performances. Indeed, Nik, who had rarely taken Betsy out anywhere after marrying her, had turned into a maddeningly visible male, whose social success was mapped by a trail of revealing photos in gossip columns and both glossy and worthy magazines.

Across the hall in the very act of emerging from Cristo's study where a couple of brandies had chased the increasing chill from his stomach, Nik had frozen into immobility at the unexpected sound of Betsy's voice. A glance at his brother revealed that even tolerant, laid-back Cristo had tensed at the obvious fact that the feisty Belle was already making dates for Nik's still legally wed wife. And with a womaniser like Chris Morrison, of all people! Only Betsy would have to ask *who* the man was! Only one of the richest bankers in the City! *Diavelos!* Nik's eyes flashed pure emerald brilliance as he fought down a tide of pure toxic rage because no matter how he felt he couldn't strangle his brother's provocative wife.

'Ah, boys together too…' Belle trilled teasingly, not one whit perturbed by the awkward meeting. 'Isn't this cosy?'

'Betsy…' Cristo gave Betsy an uneasy smile that

warned her that Nik had confided in him. She wondered if Nik's brother even appreciated how extreme an honour that was, because Nik was one of the most secretive men she had ever met. She finally dared to shift her attention to Nik. His sheer physical impact as he stood there poised with his arrogant black head held high and his broad shoulders thrown back hit her like a thunderclap. The amount of stress she had been fighting at his office had shielded her from the full effects of his compelling sexual magnetism. Now suddenly she was bare to the elements, reliving X-rated moments of their passionate encounter weeks earlier. She remembered the hard, jolting thrust of his demanding body into hers, the wild, screaming sensitivity of every nerve ending and the mad excitement that had engulfed her. A flush of heat travelled from her pelvis up through her already tender breasts and burned her face.

But behind that unwelcome response smouldered an anger and a resentment that Betsy had always repressed because as a child she had been taught to regard such emotions as destructive, rude and undesirable.

'Betsy won't need a lift from Morrison,' Nik announced, tight-mouthed. 'As I'm coming to the party as well, I'll organise her transport.'

Betsy could not credit her hearing because Nik had spoken as though she were a crate requiring shipping. Or a personal possession that he still had the right to move about at will. *This,* from a male who had deceived her, deserted her and who was racing to divorce her! Without warning a volcanic fury beyond anything Betsy had ever felt before funnelled up through her diminutive figure like hot, scorching lava and she stalked forward, blue eyes ablaze.

'Where do you get the nerve?' Betsy spat out, her small face a mask of raging indignation as she confronted Nik and jabbed a small forefinger hard into his shirtfront. 'Where the hell do you get the nerve to think you have the right to organise anything for me?'

As taken aback as if a chair had suddenly lifted up and attacked him, Nik gazed down in disbelief at Betsy, the most conciliatory person he had ever known and without an ounce of aggression, facing up to him like a miniature warrior on the battlefield.

'I—'

'Shut up…I don't want to hear your voice!' Betsy seethed up at him, head tipping back because she refused to focus on his chest, but it was a challenge to seek eye-to-eye contact when he was so much taller than she was. 'You've got nothing to say that I could possibly want to hear! You don't own me and you don't have any say in what I do or where I go or who I do it with! Only last week you were wrapped round an Amazonian blonde at some New York party. I didn't interfere. I didn't offer you an opinion. Why not? Because it was *none of my business!* And my life now is none of your business either!' she completed with a final stab of her forefinger on his broad chest. 'Do you get that, Nik? Or do I need to write it down for you, put it in business language so that you might actually grasp it?'

'That is enough,' Nik warned her, hard cheekbones rigid beneath his flushed golden skin. 'What has got into you?' he demanded, incredulous at her daring in attacking him.

'You've got into me, Nik…literally and figuratively. You were a rotten, selfish husband and you went out of my life on an even worse note—'

Cristo swung wide the door of his study in an almost comically inviting gesture. 'You and Nik can talk in there—'

'But I wouldn't miss a minute of the mouse finally roaring,' Belle confided without shame. 'You go, girl!'

Even white teeth gritting together, Nik breathed curtly, 'You're pregnant—obviously you don't want to be forced into the company of another man—'

'Why should being pregnant stop me? And who said I was being *forced*?' Betsy queried, still as furious as she had started out because Nik's many, many sins and omissions were piled up like coffin dust in the back of her mind. She wrenched her arm free the instant he closed long brown fingers round it in an effort to hustle her into the study. 'Lay one hand on me, Nik, and I'll charge you with assault—'

'You will not stage a public argument with me in my brother's house!' Nik thundered down at her, green eyes so startlingly light with rage they shimmered like polished gems in his lean dark features.

'That's fine. I wasn't planning to stay and waste my breath on a lost cause.' Azure eyes like jewels assailed his irate stare with a boldness that stunned him. 'Just don't you ever *dare* to tell me what to do again!

Subject someone else to the control-freak stuff... You're not my husband any more. I spent three years trying to be the very best wife I could be, submitting to your every demand and expectation and fitting myself into your world, and thank heaven I don't have to do it any more!' she slung at him with a sudden sense of freedom as she walked with determination towards the front door.

'We're still married,' Nik reminded her stubbornly, his attention locked to her like a powerful force beam that could not be evaded.

And Betsy spun round, rigid with so much annoyance at that provocative claim that she was instantly ready to storm into round two of the battle. '*Really?* Where have you been for the past eight months? Oh, yes, divorcing me, repossessing the dog you always ignored, trying to take the roof from over my head while running round with other women. If I did choose to sleep around, consort with lots of men and generally act like a very embarrassing ex-wife, well, I might as well, because playing nice with you all those years certainly didn't do me any favours! You lied to me—'

'I didn't... I have never *ever* lied to you,' Nik breathed grittily, big, strong hands clenched into fists by his sides, pale as death below his year-round tan. A claustrophobic silence fell while she waited to see if he would say anything else but, predictably, Nik sealed his firm masculine lips together.

'You lied by omission,' Betsy conceded and a belated flush of mortification that they were fighting in

Cristo and Belle's home engulfed her and she cringed inwardly at the lengths her loss of temper had taken her to. 'And trust you to make that distinction. You're too clever for your own good, Nik, and I was never h-half clever enough… You broke my heart, Nik, and I'll never forgive you for it.' Something very like the start of a sob clogged in her throat and her eyes burned and in more haste than ever she wrenched the front door open, starting down the steps, only halting when a heavy hand settled on her shoulder.

'Let me take you home—'

'That would be ridiculous,' she said tightly, staring fixedly out at the quiet residential street, refusing to turn her head. 'In any case my car's parked at the train station at home.'

Nik said something in Greek and a man side-stepped Betsy to yank open the passenger door of the limo parked by the kerb. One of Nik's security team, Betsy registered, her head swimming a little with the mental and physical exhaustion threatening to overwhelm her. Yet even in that condition, she couldn't help wondering and beating herself up about whether or not Nik's security men had also been witnesses to her diatribe. She had harangued Nik like a shrew, had gone up like a firework, experiencing a rage entirely new to her, and it had totally overcome her every inhibition. Sadly, in the aftermath of it, she only felt drained, ashamed and achingly weary.

Nik watched her narrow shoulders droop, her head bow, concern clawing at him even while he remained astonished by her behaviour. She had given him a glimpse into her outlook and he was reeling from it.

You broke my heart, Nik, and I'll never forgive you for it.

He turned her round, slowly, carefully. She looked up at him, eyes bright with unshed tears in the street light. His mouth came crashing down on hers without warning and suddenly he was lifting her up to him to part her soft lips and drink deep of the sweet, tender interior of her mouth. She felt as if her head were swimming as her body ran from cold to very hot and she wanted to climb him like a tree and cling. Molten desire laced with helpless self-betrayal powered her treacherous response, a wild but necessary release from the unbearable tension. He tasted so good. He tasted hotter than the flaming heart of a fire. Nothing had ever been as primitive as that devouring kiss and yet nothing could have drawn her down so efficiently from her distressed emotional high and grounded her again. He steadied her with both hands as he set her down on her own feet again because she was tottering, dizzy, in another place altogether from the mood she had been in before he reached for her.

'My car will drop you at the station… I'll stay on here,' Nik murmured in a hoarse undertone, but it was the only outward sign he gave that what had just transpired had had any kind of effect on him.

It was a huge challenge but Betsy contrived to relocate her brain and, shaken though she was, she made it down the steps, across the pavement and into the upholstered comfort of the limousine, breathing again only when the car drew away from the kerb. That kiss… No, she wasn't even going to think about that. It was just part of the craziness that happened when people lost their temper and fought and she wasn't used to fighting with Nik. Even the day she had told him to get out of Lavender Hall there had been no *real* fight. While she had ranted about the vasectomy he had kept secret he had stood in brooding silence without explaining, excusing or even attempting to justify his behaviour.

As the limo departed, it finally occurred to Nik that he had set himself much more of a challenge than he could ever have imagined. Telling Betsy that he was coming home to look after her and their unborn child would go down like a brick thrown through a glass window because *she didn't want him back.*

Returning indoors, Nik turned in a blind, unco-ordinated half circle in the hall of his brother's elegant town house and he wasn't aware of anything, of where he was or even of who might be watching for such a moment of weakness. Why had he just assumed that she would want him back? Women had always wanted Nik and it was simply a reality he took for granted. But then he had made that mistake with Betsy before when she'd ditched him on their first date, he recalled abstractedly, an iron bar pounding painfully behind his temples. Of course, Betsy had never been like other women, which was why he had married her in the first place.

When he had brought her flowers she had admitted she would simply prefer an apology for his long absences and more frequent phone calls and texts while he was away.

When he had brought her gifts she had scolded him for wasting his money as if he were an extravagant child. *'You can't impress me with that stuff,'* she had once told him gently. *'That's not why I'm with you. I'm here because I love you and you can't put a price on that.'*

Perspiration dampening his brow, Nik asked himself for the first time why Betsy had tried to claim half his wealth, because that claim from her had never made sense with what he knew of her character. He wondered what love really felt like, never having experienced it except when it came to her loving him. That love had given him the strangest sense of security... Ridiculous! As if he were *insecure*. He almost laughed out loud at that idea but somehow couldn't crank up even a shadowy atom of his sense of humour.

He wondered if it would be possible to kidnap Betsy and take her abroad where she would have to listen to him. Would she really call the police? Ultimately, she *had* to listen to him. Catching himself up on that peculiar kidnapping fantasy, he raised his brows and wondered if he had taken a sudden nosedive into insanity.

Like Betsy, acting so oddly, attacking him like that. What was the matter with her? Was it possible that it had only happened because she was pregnant? How had he forgotten that for even as long as five minutes? Pregnant ladies had to be very hormonal, he

FREE Merchandise is 'in the Cards' for you!

Dear Reader,

We're giving away FREE MERCHANDISE!

Seriously, we'd like to reward you for reading this novel by giving you **FREE MERCHANDISE** worth over $20. And no purchase is necessary!

You see the Jack of Hearts sticker above? Paste that sticker in the box on the Free Merchandise Voucher inside. Return the Voucher promptly...and we'll send you valuable Free Merchandise!

Thanks again for reading one of our novels—and enjoy your Free Merchandise with our compliments!

Pam Powers

Pam Powers

P.S. Look inside to see what Free Merchandise is **"in the cards"** for you!

YOUR FREE MERCHANDISE INCLUDES...

2 FREE Books **AND** 2 FREE Mystery Gifts

▶ Detach card and mail today. No stamp needed. ▶

FREE MERCHANDISE VOUCHER

2 FREE BOOKS and 2 FREE GIFTS

Please send my Free Merchandise, consisting of **2 Free Books** and **2 Free Mystery Gifts**. I understand that I am under no obligation to buy anything, as explained on the back of this card.

❏ I prefer the regular-print edition
106/306 HDL GEHZ

❏ I prefer the larger-print edition
176/376 HDL GEHZ

Please Print

FIRST NAME

LAST NAME

ADDRESS

APT.#   CITY

STATE/PROV.   ZIP/POSTAL CODE

NO PURCHASE NECESSARY!

HP-714-FM13

thought vaguely. Betsy had definitely not been herself; in fact she had behaved like someone possessed, displaying a change of character he was happy to lay at argumentative Belle's door. After all, he knew that Belle didn't like him and was likely to use his worst mistakes and flaws against him. Although, Nik reasoned with a frown, it was more probable that the only demon possessing Betsy was the result of unstable pregnancy hormones. He was more than a little relieved to have worked out that obvious explanation. That raving virago of a woman had borne no resemblance whatsoever to the soft and gentle Betsy he had once lived with. And would be living with again soon, Nik reminded himself with satisfaction.

Betsy would be surprised but pleased, ultimately *very* pleased, he told himself with charged conviction. Since the day Betsy had told him to get out of Lavender Hall, Nik had been pursued and propositioned by other women on a daily basis. He had met with seductive looks and bold advances everywhere he went and after three years of marriage such bold invites had proved disconcerting and a passion killer, but, even so, if other women who didn't even know him could want him so much that they dropped all finesse and dignity, Betsy must want him back more, mustn't she?

She had let him take her up against the wall that day. Just thinking about it, Nik got hard as steel. She couldn't honestly hate him if she had had sex with him again, could she? Why the hell was he thinking about all this stupid relationship stuff? For a split second of seething frustration Nik wanted to bang his head on the wall to clear it of the chaotic madness of his thoughts and then he finally registered his brother's presence several feet away.

'Are you OK?' Cristo was watching him worriedly.

Nik flexed his stiff shoulders and straightened to his full height. 'Why wouldn't I be?'

Cristo was not subtle but he knew that telling Nik he was acting weird would be more of a hindrance than a help. In any case Cristo was operating in full sympathy mode. Nik had married a mouse who had started roaring like a lion and naturally he couldn't cope with that unnerving switch of personality on top of the prospect of a baby as well.

Nik was very much a man's man, short on the imagination and empathy stakes, Cristo thought understandingly. Cristo had long since noticed that in complete contrast to his brother's brilliant intellect and polished business negotiation skills, Nik was downright backward and all at sea when anything emotional got involved in a situation. But Nik was trying to understand; Cristo could see quite clearly that Nik was *trying* and struggling, and he just hoped that, sooner rather than later, Betsy would see it too.

CHAPTER SIX

IT WAS EARLY evening and Betsy was staring down the front steps at the huge removal van and the crew standing beside it and said for the second time, 'Obviously you've got the address wrong. I'm not moving any place and nobody is moving in…'

Simultaneously with that statement came the loud thwack-thwack of rotor blades sounding overhead and drowning out her words. Everyone, including Betsy, looked up into the sky but only Betsy was in a position to identify the logo on the helicopter coming in to land on the helipad Nik had had built. Betsy blinked, blindsided by yet another baffling event. Was Nik flying in to visit her? To discuss the baby and future arrangements between them? But why wouldn't he have done that through the medium of their respective legal advisors? Surely that would have been less challenging than yet another traumatic meeting?

Five days had passed since Betsy had confronted Nik in Cristo and Belle's home and she was still cringing, inwardly raging and squirming at the memory of how she had finally given her almost ex-husband a few much-needed home truths. It was unfortunate that she had done that in front of an audience; indeed she felt she owed Nik an apology on that score for having lost control to that extent. On the other hand, Nik was not given to introspection and had probably shaken off her criticisms within minutes of her departure. He wasn't a sensitive male and he didn't love her, so why should he care about what she had said about the past when their marriage was over, barring the final legal ratification? And why the heck had he kissed her afterwards? What kind of sense had that move made?

Sky-blue eyes opening very wide, Betsy watched Nik striding through the shrubbery that concealed the helipad and her blood ran cold as she worried again about what might have prompted him to make yet another personal visit. He delegated responsibility whenever he could to free himself up for the much more stimulating arena of the business world.

She concentrated on guiltily trying not to notice how amazing Nik looked in his charcoal-grey designer suit, how exotically, wonderfully handsome with that luxuriant black hair and those stunning light eyes of his that were so striking against his bronzed skin. Her colour fluctuated, her chilled blood started heating up dangerously in her veins and she wanted to slap herself for reacting to his compelling sexual charisma even after all he had done to her. It was just stupid chemistry, she told herself in exasperation. That was why, in a nutshell, she had kissed him back that night; it was a sad fact of life but she found him utterly irresistible.

She was surprised when Nik paused at the rear of the removals van to address the hovering work crew and wondered what he was saying to them. At least as a male with very little patience for inefficiency and other people's mistakes, he would soon send them about their business.

'Betsy…' Nik purred, mounting the steps in a couple of graceful strides of his long, powerful legs, his jewelled gaze locking to hers like a guided missile trained on a target, she thought dimly, little hot and cold tremors winging through her in an unnerving wave of response.

'What are you doing here?' Betsy asked, striving this time around to be cool and sensible in her reaction to his arrival. 'Couldn't you at least have called to say that you were coming?'

A hairy mop of dog provided an interruption by hurling himself cheerfully against Nik's legs in welcome.

'Gizmo…' Betsy scolded.

'He must like having us both in the same place again,' Nik pronounced, actually laughing and reaching down to pet a flyaway doggy ear.

'Well, he'll be disappointed then when you leave again,' Betsy remarked tightly. 'Honestly, Nik, you should've phoned to at least mention that you would be visiting—'

Nik frowned. 'Could we have a word in private?' he was careful to enquire.

Glancing behind him, her brow furrowing in be-
musement when she registered that the removal men
were actually opening up the back of their lumbering
behemoth of a truck, Betsy murmured, 'Of course.
Has something happened?'

'Nothing you need to worry about,' Nik asserted, a
lean brown hand settling into the indent of her slender
spine as he urged her in the direction of the drawing
room and, having got her there, he prudently closed
the door.

'So, something *has* happened,' Betsy assumed,
searching his lean, darkly beautiful features, recognising his tension and constraint in growing dismay.

Nik breathed in slow and deep. Moving back in
had seemed so simple a solution when he had thought
of it but, faced with Betsy's sheer bewilderment at his
appearance, it suddenly seemed rather more complicated than that. Cristo had urged him to go and talk
to her first but Nik had wanted to avoid drama and
the unthinkable possibility of rejection. Presenting
Betsy with a fait accompli and checking out his legal
position in advance had impressed him as a more
workable and efficient approach. After all, he didn't
warn a company that he was about to take over what
he was planning to do in advance, did he?

'Why aren't you saying anything? You're scaring
me... What's wrong?' Betsy gasped, her nervous tension reaching an unbelievable high. 'Are Cristo and
Belle all right?'

'Of course they are.' Nik scanned his wife in a
swift all-over appraisal that missed not a single de-

tail of her jeans-clad, relaxed appearance. She still didn't look pregnant and he wondered when her tiny, slender proportions would show change. He glanced away, colour lining his cheekbones, marvelling at the amount of instant hunger coursing through him. Evidently she owned the key to his libido, or perhaps it was just that he was an exceptionally faithful married man with some mental kink that had prevented him from seeking release with another woman even during a legal separation. With some relief he reached for that practical explanation.

'Nik…what is it?' Betsy pressed worriedly, stiff as a walking stick as she stood in front of him.

'I'm moving back in.' Nik let the announcement hang there and watched Betsy's mouth fall open to display two rows of small pearly-white teeth. 'I've decided to come home—'

Betsy almost fell over in shock. In fact her head swam and her ears buzzed as those words rhymed back and forth inside her head and she refused to credit them. 'I beg your pardon?' she said limply.

'I want to come home,' Nik spelt out in case she had yet to get the message. 'Make a go of our marriage again…'

He's certifiably insane, Betsy decided dizzily. The last time he had seen her she had been screaming at him and now, all of a sudden and without the smallest warning, he was telling her he wanted to come back and live with her again. And, worst of all, he spoke as if such a far-reaching decision were entirely one-sided and his alone to make.

'You mean…that removal van out there—?'

'*Ne*…yes. It's mine,' Nik admitted, relieved that she had finally understood without him having to spell anything out in greater or potentially embarrassing detail. 'Don't worry, you won't be put out in any way. I called Edna and warned her—'

'You phoned our housekeeper to tell her you were moving back in and *you didn't tell me?*' Betsy demanded in a charged voice, thinking that the arrival of his possessions was a great deal less perplexing than his own arrival, only he didn't seem to grasp that obvious little fact.

'Only an hour ago,' Nik confided as though that might mitigate the offence.

Betsy breathed in so deep that her head swam again and she studied him in disbelief. 'Nik…you can't just decide you want to try again at our marriage without discussing it first with me,' she pointed out a little shakily, hysteria gathering somewhere deep inside her chest because she just could not believe what she was hearing.

'I'm discussing it with you now,' Nik countered levelly, strolling over to the blazing fire. 'I want you to be pleased.'

It wasn't the first time in their relationship Nik had told her how she ought to feel before she could decide on her own account, so she wasn't surprised by that seemingly careless aside. 'Nik…you left eight months ago. This is my house and home now—'

Nik swung back round, lean, strong face taut. 'No,

it's not. The settlement papers have yet to be signed. The hall still belongs to me—'

'Oh, that's all right, then,' Betsy told him with spirited sarcasm. 'I'll just pack up me and Gizmo and sleep on Belle's couch! I'm sure she'll squeeze us in somewhere—'

'What on earth are you talking about?' Nik demanded darkly. 'Why would you leave now that I've moved back in again?'

'We are getting a divorce, Nik,' Betsy reminded him doggedly, wondering on what planet his reasoning had been formed. 'You *can't* just move back in and spring a reconciliation on me without my agreement—'

'I don't want a divorce. We have a son or a daughter on the way and we should be together to raise him or her,' Nik informed her without fanfare.

'Ideally speaking…' Betsy commented weakly. 'I had no idea you felt that way about the baby when you never wanted one.'

'But the baby's now a fact of life,' Nik replied. 'We're going to be parents and I won't allow my child to grow up without me.'

Betsy was afraid her legs would give out as support and she sidled over to a sofa and literally dropped down on it in a desperate attempt to clear her light-headedness. 'Nik? All this is coming at me out of nowhere and I'm very confused—'

'Why?' Nik queried with apparent sincerity, crossing the rug to crouch down at her feet so that he could still see her face. 'I'm home again—'

'But that's not a unilateral decision you can make!' Betsy exclaimed in a raw outburst. '*Obviously* it concerns me as well. I know it's best for a child to have two parents if possible but there's the question of *our* relationship—'

His wide, sensual mouth quirked. 'There wouldn't be a child to worry about in the first instance if it wasn't for our relationship.'

'Depends on how you look at the situation.' Betsy lifted her head, cobalt eyes sparking with annoyance. 'I saw it as just sex and straight afterwards you did as well when you said that you believed it was quite common for divorcing couples to fall into bed together again.'

'It was the wrong thing to say.' Nik raked restive brown fingers through his silky black hair as he made that confession. 'But I was…er…very confused that day. I didn't know what I felt or what to say to you—'

Betsy found herself strangely touched by that uncharacteristically frank admission but it did not silence her. 'No, you just *ran*—'

Nik's green eyes flared with macho male defensiveness. 'I did *not* run—'

'Take it from me…you *ran* as if I was a one-night stand you regretted. Only a week ago you were divorcing me. How can you go from that level to suddenly saying you want to be married to me again?' she prompted shakily.

Nik paced restively in front of the fire because he hadn't expected so many questions or the barrier of resistance she was engaged in raising between them. But she wasn't screaming at him, which he deemed a plus and an improvement. 'You have to start somewhere—'

'But all that's changed is that I'm pregnant,' Betsy reminded him, trying not to listen to the opening and closing of doors in the hall and the sound of voices and noise that accompanied Nik's possessions returning to what had once been the home they shared. She was traumatised and trying not to show it. Not for the first time, Nik's conduct had stunned her into silence. He had stopped the divorce, returned to her... But why? She didn't understand. 'I can't believe that you care that much about a baby you never wanted—'

Nik tensed. *'Believe,'* he urged. 'I also care about you and I want to be here for both you and the baby now and in the future.'

'It's an amazing turnaround,' Betsy told him numbly. 'I don't know how I feel about it.'

Nik hunkered down athletically again at her feet and reached for both her hands in an unusual demonstration for a male who was normally very reserved. 'Be pleased. I want to come home, *glikia mou.* I suppose I'm asking you for a second chance...'

It was so humble, so unlike the proud, fiercely independent male she knew that tears stung the backs of Betsy's clear eyes. She stared at him, her gaze locked to the sleek, dark, fallen-angel beauty of his lean, taut face and she could literally sense how keyed up he was waiting for her to agree. It meant a great deal to him; she could *feel* that. And she thought that only a male of Nik Christakis's complexity could think it was normal to move back in with the wife he was divorcing without even talking the idea over with her in advance. There had always been something about his sheer lack of emotional intelligence that pierced her heart deep as an arrow. He was so clever but so out of touch with ordinary things that she took for granted and she had always recognised that eccentric quality in him, right from the night of his equally startling wedding proposal, which had also come out of nowhere at her.

'I'm not sure I could trust you again,' she told him honestly. 'So much has happened…and the other women—'

'I haven't slept with anyone but you.'

Betsy was astonished until she recalled him falling on her like a hungry wolf and it was that recollection that convinced her that he was telling the truth. 'Even so, you've been photographed out and about with a lot of other women—'

'But I've only been with you,' Nik declared afresh. 'I only *want* to be with you.'

Betsy lifted uncertain fingers and traced his darkly shadowed jawline, fingertips brushing the stubble already formed there. She wondered what she was doing. But she was realising that her supposed hatred of Nik had only provided a useful bolster to her pride and her survival, and that when she went looking for its strength to stiffen her spine with resistance, it was mysteriously absent. She didn't hate him; she wanted him back. Did that make her the biggest female fool in the Western world? Was she crazy to even consider reconciling with a guy who arrived with a removals van as if eight months of separation and all the bitter turns and twists of the divorce proceedings had never happened?

'But you *never* wanted a baby,' she heard herself remind him hoarsely.

'A child is a big responsibility,' Nik said seriously, evidently indifferent to the reality that he already had responsibility for a vast business empire and thousands and thousands of employees round the world. 'And children are very vulnerable. That was why I never wanted the responsibility of protecting one.'

Betsy didn't follow his reasoning. He seemed to be thinking of some kind of doomsday scenario in which a child could get hurt, but she could see that he was deadly serious and for that reason she nodded as if she totally understood what he was saying. 'And that's why you had the vasectomy?' she prompted.

Nik nodded in silence, having given the explanation that he had already worked out beforehand. He wished he could have come up with those words eight months earlier when it might have saved them both a lot of grief. But at the time, in shock at her discovery that he had had a vasectomy, he had thought he could only tell her the truth and that was an option he could not even contemplate, would *never* contemplate.

Betsy searched his lean dark face, noticed the shadows below his eyes, the indented lines of extreme tension bracketing his mouth, and tried to think straight. But with no warning whatsoever, emotional overload and exhaustion were together hitting her like a freight train hurtling downhill. 'I can't give you an answer right now,' she told him shakily. 'I need to think about it and I think I need to lie down for a while…'

Rigid with dissatisfaction at that response, Nik backed away as Betsy levered herself upright and then, without a jot of warning, her eyes rolled up in her head and she just dropped where she stood without a sound. Betsy had fainted. There was something seriously wrong with her. Nik, usually ice cool in a crisis, experienced an intense wave of panic as he scooped her up and strode out to the hall again, where their housekeeper, Edna, was supervising the removal team.

'Oh, dear, has Mrs Christakis fainted again?' Edna prompted in a mild tone of acceptance as she moved towards him.

'*Again?* You mean this has happened before?' Nik pressed in consternation.

'Some women are prone to it in early pregnancy,' the older woman told him calmly. 'We all watch out for her as best we can.'

Nik pictured Betsy fainting as she crossed a road and falling beneath the wheels of a car. He saw her tumbling downstairs and breaking her neck. Even when he envisaged her falling and simply bruising herself he felt sick, and determined that it wasn't going to happen any more. Having a baby could kill her, he reflected in horror. He couldn't have her fainting all over the place; it was too dangerous, too risky.

He needed proper medical advice and somewhere to keep her safe.

Betsy drifted back to consciousness to find that she was lying across Nik's lap in the back of a limousine. 'Where on earth are we going?' she whispered, her fingers fluttering up to brush her clammy brow. 'I did it again, didn't I? Sometimes if I stand up too fast I pass out. Sorry if I gave you a fright. I'm just so tired—'

'I'm taking you to see a doctor—'

'That's not necessary—'

'When you're ill *I* decide what's necessary.'

'But I'm not ill. I'm only pregnant,' Betsy countered gently, recognising his concern and his stress level. Nik did not like the unexpected. In the same way she knew that every piece of furniture he had taken with him would be returned to pretty much the same position it had occupied eight months earlier. He had a thing about familiar order and structure, which had once thoroughly irritated her because she liked to move stuff around and try it in different places. But then everyone had their little quirks and preferences, she conceded ruefully.

'I think you need to rest,' Nik spelt out.

Her nose was almost buried in his shirtfront and the musky, sexy scent of his skin was so familiar it made her eyes prickle with tears. Her fingers clenched round the front edge of his jacket and she lowered her lids. She loved him but that didn't mean she could live with him again or raise their child with him. It would mean a return to being a business widow because he would always be travelling, unavailable when she needed and wanted him. It would be lonely and thankless because he wouldn't appreciate how much she missed him. Their child would hardly see him, would even struggle to recognise him when he was away for weeks on end. Was a part-time father better than none at all?

Odd electronic beeps and loud voices roused her again.

'Betsy, tell them that you know where you're going,' Nik instructed, turning up her face to horrendously bright lights so that she shut her eyes fast again.

''Course I do,' she mumbled, willing to say anything if it meant being left in peace again.

'My wife can't help being unwell,' he breathed, anger in his voice now fracturing his Greek accent as he tightened his arms round her.

Her head was pounding and the familiar weariness settled back over her like a blanketing fog because it had been so many long weeks since she had enjoyed a decent night's sleep. She blocked the anxious thoughts battering to be heard inside her heavy head; she would think through all the complexities of her marriage and Nik with a clearer head some other day...

Betsy shifted on the comfortable mattress and a low sigh escaped her as she opened her eyes on the shadowy room. There was a low drone in the background. 'What's that noise?' she mumbled sleepily.

'Go back to sleep… It's late,' Nik advised from the foot of the bed. 'I shouldn't have come in but I wanted to check on you… Instead I'm afraid I woke you up.'

Remembering what had happened earlier, Betsy tensed, her gaze darting round what little she could see of the dim and seemingly quite small room. She could only assume she was in one of Nik's guest rooms in London. Where else would he take her to see a doctor? And why hadn't she argued, for goodness' sake? Because arguing with Nik had always been pointless. When Nik was convinced that he was doing something in her best interests he was impossible to shift.

'Why were you checking up on me?' she framed.

Unshaven and decidedly tousled with his black hair ruffled and his tie and jacket missing, Nik loomed large as a twenty-storey building, poised beside the bed. 'You collapsed,' he reminded her almost accusingly. 'That's not normal—'

'I had a silly little faint…more embarrassing than serious,' Betsy fielded sleepily, realising that for some reason she felt strangely soothed by his presence.

'You seem to be incredibly tired—'

'I haven't been sleeping well recently,' Betsy admitted before she could think better of that revealing confession. 'And fatigue is normal in the early stages of pregnancy.'

'The doctor will tell us tomorrow what's normal and what is cause for concern.'

'It's not like you to fuss over something trivial—'

'The state of your health is not a triviality.'

He sounded so serious that a drowsy smile of amusement lit her tired face before she shut her eyes again.

Betsy wakened to light flooding through a porthole window and blinked in confusion. She clambered slowly out of bed and, even before she reached the window to get a good view of the clouds beyond it, she knew she was on board a plane. The lights that had blinded her the night before, the questions Nik had been angrily parrying, must have taken place at airport security the night before. How stupid am I? she asked herself in consternation. Why am I on a plane? Why did he put me on a plane without mentioning it? But then why did Nik *do* anything?

The clothes she had been wearing were in the wardrobe but she was relieved to find that a selection of other items had evidently been packed for her and she yanked out fresh underwear before rushing impatiently into the en suite to freshen up. The discovery of her toiletries and her make-up bag did nothing to mollify her. She felt like Alice in Wonderland, only, instead of her falling, Nik had *thrown* her down the rabbit hole. The bright blue sky beyond the porthole persuaded her to choose a light floral skirt and tee from the sparse selection of clothing and, dressed, she walked out into the main cabin with the light of battle in her eyes.

Nik was working at a laptop for all the world as though he were in an office. He glanced up through lush black lashes, green eyes gleaming. 'I heard you get up. Breakfast should be here soon—'

'Where on earth are we?'

'In thirty minutes we'll be landing in Athens—'

'Athens?' Betsy yelled.

'I told you that I was taking you to a doctor. Mikis Xenophon is the world's leading authority on pregnant women,' Nik informed her with distinct satisfaction. 'And you have an appointment with him this morning—'

'I don't care who the heck he is!' Betsy shot back at him, out of all patience. 'I was willing to see a doctor but I wasn't willing to fly to Greece to do it!'

'Xenophon is the best. I want you to see the best,' Nik countered stubbornly. 'His research is first class and his patients speak very highly of him—'

'But bringing me to Greece without *asking* me,' Betsy began half an octave higher.

'You fell very deeply asleep. You must've badly needed the rest. I was determined not to disturb you,' Nik assured her tautly.

At that point a knock sounded on the door and the breakfast he had ordered arrived. Expelling her pent-up breath in a rush, Betsy sat down because, having missed dinner the night before, she was truly hungry. But as she nibbled she quietly seethed in frustration. He had done it again, taken over, steamrollering over her options and wishes as if only he knew best. The one and only occasion when he had ever let her choose anything had been the time when he had finally agreed that she could try for a baby if she wanted to. Of course that had been a safe choice from his point of view when he had known that his vasectomy had meant that there was then no prospect of her falling pregnant.

'Why on earth did you ever agree to me trying to get pregnant last year?' Betsy found herself asking him abruptly. 'I mean, when you knew it *couldn't* happen, why did you give way?'

Unprepared for the question, Nik stared fixedly back at her. 'I thought it would satisfy you. I…incorrectly, perhaps even foolishly, assumed you'd go off the idea again… After all, you didn't want children when we got married and somehow I never expected that to change—'

'Unfortunately, people do change. I thought I didn't want children because my parents never really wanted me—that was a major turn-off. I also spent a lot of time helping to look after the younger kids when I was a teenager in the foster system and I saw kids back then as nothing more than a time-consuming responsibility who stole away your freedom,' Betsy explained ruefully. 'I genuinely didn't *ever* expect to start wanting a baby, but I was too young when I made that decision and shared it with you.'

Nik nodded grimly. 'I will give you that. So, what changed?'

Her small face stiffened. 'You were away on business so much. I was bored, lonely, and then one day I woke up and somehow I believed a baby would be the best thing that ever happened to me and that everything would be improved with a child in the picture.'

'But you became obsessed by your desire for a child.' Nik sighed. 'I'm afraid I didn't understand how

important having a baby had come to mean to you…
that it was as much an emotional as a physical desire.'

Betsy tore her croissant into at least ten pieces
and then began buttering each one while deciding
that nothing less than honesty would suffice. 'Yes, I
was obsessed,' she agreed, thinking back to the vita-
mins she had taken, the temperature charts to check
when she was ovulating, the acupuncture and yoga
sessions, the state of mind and pure desperation that
had persuaded her that she would do literally *anything* to become pregnant.

Nik hadn't expected her to admit that. 'I felt shut
out and extremely uncomfortable because I knew that
no matter what you did it would be in vain.'

'Obviously,' Betsy conceded, glad to hear that guilt
had afflicted him even if he didn't have the right word
to quantify the feeling.

'I assumed you would just give up and forget about
it eventually,' he admitted with what would have been
poignant ignorance had it only related to a less sensitive subject.

'No, what you can't have, you just want *more,*'
Betsy whispered ruefully.

And now she had finally got it and she was almost
in Greece and Nik was back in her life. Was that what
she wanted? Betsy was ashamed to realise that she
truly didn't know any more. Her troubled gaze rested
on him, skimming over his bold bronzed profile before skipping down the long, straight slope of his
perfect nose to linger on the full curve of his sensual
mouth, and as if aware of her scrutiny he turned his

handsome dark head. Eyes that were glittering slivers of bright green ringed by luxuriant black lashes transfixed her with stunning effect. Her mouth ran dry and her tummy flipped a helpless somersault.

But that was her body reacting, not her mind, Betsy reasoned shamefacedly. Sadly, her brain was going round and round in ever-shrinking circles without reaching any definitive conclusion and it had been doing that for weeks. What did she want? Could she forgive him? *Was* he sincere? How could he simply walk away and then walk back? Could he *really* care about their baby's future? And what about her? Her needs? Her wants? Her happiness?

CHAPTER SEVEN

MR XENOPHON PLEATED his fingers and surveyed his anxious patient and her even more anxious husband. He had run a battery of standard tests and reached certain obvious conclusions.

'You are *very* stressed, Mrs Christakis,' he told Betsy gently. 'And although you don't yet seem to be aware of the fact, you are carrying twins. A twin pregnancy will be a heavier burden—'

'She's *stressed*?' Nik demanded as if the concept was entirely foreign to him.

'You are both very stressed,' the doctor pronounced mildly. 'Why is not my concern but you both need to find some way of reducing that stress for the sake of your wife's health.'

Betsy finally unpeeled her tongue from the roof of her mouth. 'I'm expecting…*twins?*' she finally pressed for clarification.

'My grandfather was a twin,' Nik commented, very much in the tone of someone owning up to a regrettable secret.

Not one but *two* babies, Betsy reflected in a daze.

Nik was probably filled with horror at the prospect of what might well strike him as a positive *horde* of babies.

'Mrs Christakis is in poor condition right now for a twin pregnancy, which will demand more of her and her body,' Mr Xenophon informed them calmly before focusing his attention on Betsy to continue. 'You are underweight even for your petite frame. You are anaemic. Clearly, you're not eating enough for a pregnant lady who needs all her strength. Your blood pressure is not good either. It's not bad but it is not what it should be. Thankfully, all those problems are easily curable with a sensible approach. The stress is most probably causing the rise in your blood pressure but you need to find your own solution to dealing with that. It should involve lots of rest and reasonable exercise. There is a higher risk of premature birth with twins. You must both make the mother-to-be's health your top priority.'

While listening, Nik had slowly lost all his natural colour. It was beginning to sink in to him that just being pregnant could be dangerous, seriously dangerous, for a woman's health. The mere idea of anything happening to Betsy sent a queasy roll through his stomach and he swallowed hard. 'Whatever it takes to improve Betsy's state of health, it will be done.'

'Twins,' Betsy mused in a complete stupor as they emerged onto the sunlit pavement to climb back into the waiting limousine. 'I saw the nurse pointing during the scan but, of course, I couldn't understand what she was saying. Didn't you?'

'I wasn't looking at the screen or listening. I was looking at you because you looked so worried—'

'I never dreamt... *Twins!* I mean, I've barely changed shape—'

The concept of *two* babies battling to occupy Betsy's tiny, fragile body at one and the same time only filled Nik with guilt and fear. Had he been more careful, had he thought to use precautions, had he suppressed his desire for her, none of this would have happened, he acknowledged angrily. But then, had she not fallen pregnant, would he have her back in his life? He thought not. And oddly enough, that acknowledgement banished all the razor-edged regrets attacking him.

Cristo's wife, Belle, phoned when they were walking back through the airport.

'Where the heck have you been?'

'Greece. Nik flew me to Athens to see an obstetrician.'

'As you do,' Belle mocked after a disconcerted pause. 'When will you be home?'

Betsy asked Nik. He veiled his gaze. 'I don't plan for us to return immediately,' he admitted. 'After what the doctor said I thought a week of rest and relaxation here would be a wiser idea... What do you think?'

The addition of the 'what do you think?' question was a groundbreaking improvement from Nik's domineering corner.

'I'll phone you later,' Betsy told her sister-in-law,

and in the VIP travel lounge she sat down beside her husband. 'Where are you planning on taking me?'

'The island of Vesos, where I spent my first years in my grandfather's home.'

Betsy hadn't known even that small fact about his childhood and even had she been furious with him, which for once she was not, she would not have missed the chance to see the island. In any case she knew Nik well enough to recognise that he was seriously worried about her physical condition and the doctor's sober pronouncements had filled her with dismay and guilt as well. Obviously she had not been looking after herself and her pregnancy as well as she had dimly imagined.

She felt humbled by that knowledge. After all, she had longed to have a child for so long and here she was gifted with the prospect of two babies and her body wasn't doing the job it should be doing because she had stressed and fretted, skipped meals and lain awake too many nights. Now she felt duly punished and arguing with Nik was the last thing on her mind. Indeed she was willing to do virtually anything to get her blood pressure back to normal and her condition improved to the level where she could carry a twin pregnancy safely to term.

'How on earth will Alice cope without me?' Betsy groaned. 'There's deliveries arriving every day—'

'I've already instructed her to hire temporary help to provide cover during your absence.'

'You think of everything—'

'No, I don't. If I did, we wouldn't be in this situation now. Xenophon was right. We're both stressed out of our minds. The divorce, the unexpected pregnancy, the constant conflict,' Nik bit out in a tone of harsh regret. 'How could we be anything else but stressed?'

'I'm going to be a lot more sensible,' Betsy swore.

'And instead of playing points, I will do what I can to support you, *glikia mou*.'

Nik lifted Betsy out of the helicopter as though she were fashioned of spun glass and Betsy suppressed a groan of frustration. Nik in rare conscience-stricken mode was entertaining for a while but she was convinced that the lion's share of the problems she was suffering were down to her own obstinate refusal to make adjustments to her schedule. She hadn't felt well but she had kept on pushing herself, determined to maintain the same workload and hours, refusing to consider that her condition might force changes on her usual routine. After all, she knew that most women worked through their pregnancies and had assumed she would be no different, but perhaps she ought to have sought medical advice when the fainting had started and she had realised that she was feeling consistently under par.

Nik set her down below the pine trees, where she breathed in the salt-laden air with a helpless sigh of pleasure and stood gazing down the grassed slope to the pale glistening stretch of beach washed by the surf. 'It's beautiful. Where do we stay?'

'I built a house here.'

'Did you? I assumed you had inherited your grandfather's home,' she said in surprise.

When she glanced at him enquiringly, his lean dark features were clenched hard, his eyes shuttered. 'I signed it over to my mother, although island life is too quiet for her tastes and I have been told that she only makes occasional use of the property. We flew over it coming in. It's that sprawling marble monstrosity on the cliffs. Did you notice it?'

'Yes...the villa with the massive pool area?'

Tight-mouthed, he nodded confirmation with a jerk of his stubborn chin and splayed a hand to the base of her slender spine to lead her through the trees. 'Lunch should be waiting for us. I want you to eat and go straight to bed—'

'I'm not an invalid. You know, you never even mentioned that you owned a house here in Greece,' Betsy reminded him as the trees slowly thinned out and an ultra-modern and graceful white villa surrounded by gloriously colourful gardens appeared in front of them. 'Especially one so beautiful. Why didn't you suggest we come here for our honeymoon?'

Nik gritted his even white teeth together, reluctant to admit that his memories of his time on the island had haunted him for years. 'I originally built the house solely as an investment I intended to sell but I never got around to it. To be frank, I left the island to go to boarding school and, after my grandfather died, I had no good reason to return here—'

'So not much in the way of sentimental attachment to this place, then?' Betsy guessed, recognising the taut flex of long fingers against her spine, aware that he was very uneasy beneath the barrage of her questions and wondering why.

But then that was Nik, a fascinatingly complex male, layered with mystery with nothing as you expected and no information granted for free. It had always been that way and she had learned to live with that wall of reserve. When they were first married she had walked in awe of him and his achievements, unable to understand why such a magnificently handsome, clever and wealthy male should choose to marry a lowly waitress when he might have married some rich socialite or successful businesswoman instead. She had never stopped being grateful that he had picked her, which was why she had never felt she had the right to complain when he left her alone so much.

Every paradise has thorns, she had thought, striving to be practical, knowing that many women would have been content simply to have a beautiful home and a string of credit cards at their disposal. Loving him to distraction, however, had made Betsy much greedier for his time and attention. Unfortunately she didn't think any human being would ever engage his interest to the extent that his business empire did, and wishing for more from him was like wishing for the moon.

Even so, it was unfortunate that Nik's former inability to grant her much of his personal time should have reminded Betsy of her years in foster care, when she had never been anyone's priority and her needs had been more often a second thought rather than a first. Nik had left her isolated at Lavender Hall, much as she had been isolated in a series of foster homes without close connections to the other inhabitants or loving carers. In those days, she had wondered if she was inherently unlovable.

They walked into a cool white hall, decorated with lush plants, to be greeted by a pleasant middle-aged housekeeper called Stephania. At the foot of the winding elegant staircase, Nik bent and lifted Betsy into his arms, ignoring her protests.

'No stairs for you,' he pronounced drily. 'If a dizzy spell hit you at the wrong moment you could have a nasty accident.'

'You always think in worst-case scenarios,' Betsy censured, amazed by the level of his pessimism while looking up at him to marvel at the length and lushness of his eyelashes, amused that she had to wear falsies to get even a hint of such luxuriance. It was wasted on him too, she thought abstractedly, for he was the least vain man she knew.

'No, I'm taking sensible precautions for your benefit,' Nik countered, reaching the wide decorative landing without an iota of breathlessness. But then in the wake of the doctor's comments, Betsy didn't think that carrying her could offer a well-built male much of a challenge.

The bedroom was a huge, dreamy space furnished with pale oak furniture, natural stone walls and draperies fluttering lightly at the open windows. Nik rested her down on a wide, sumptuously dressed bed.

Betsy rested her head approvingly back on a crisp white linen pillow. 'This place reminds me of a five-star boutique hotel.'

Nik slipped off her shoes and a knock sounded on the door to herald the entrance of a maid with a tray. Betsy sat up against the banked pillows while Nik collected the tray. He handed her a fork and sat down on the side of the bed. 'Eat before you sleep,' he urged.

It was a chicken casserole and very good but his reference to sleep had roused her interest. 'I was just wondering,' Betsy began abruptly, putting curiosity ahead of tact when it came to what had once been a touchy subject. 'Do you still suffer from the nightmares you used to get?'

Before her very eyes, Nik stiffened defensively, his bright eyes immediately veiling. 'No. It seems that was just a phase. I was working too hard last year, not allowing myself enough downtime to chill,' he parried with resolute cool.

'You never would tell me what the nightmares were about,' Betsy could not resist reminding him.

Nik shrugged a broad shoulder with careful unconcern. 'Telling you about them would have given them undue importance and lodged them in my mind even deeper,' he proffered in explanation. 'I have always preferred not to dwell on negative events.'

He had removed his jacket and tie. Lean muscles flexed beneath his silk shirt as he reached for the tray when she finished eating and set it aside. He closed his hand over hers. 'Now, you go to sleep.'

While she studied him with wondering blue eyes,

his thumb caressed the soft inner skin of her wrist in a soothing motion and he lifted her hand, spread her fingers and pressed a kiss to her palm.

Her heart thumped in the smouldering silence, gooseflesh erupting on her exposed skin, tiny hairs rising at the nape of her neck while low in her pelvis she felt the sweet, all-pervasive tug of the hunger that only he could stir. Her breath shortened in her throat as she stared back at him. It was no use, his gut-wrenching sensuality plundered her defences like an invading army. That fast she wanted his mouth, wanted his hands on her body…and a great deal more. Colour blooming in her cheeks, she felt her nipples strain and push against the bodice of her dress while her thighs pressed together to ease the ache he had induced at the heart of her.

'Later,' Nik breathed with hoarse emphasis, sexual anticipation written boldly in every line of his hard, angular features and the blaze of his eyes. 'If you sleep now, I'll make a late-night banquet of you.'

Betsy was taken aback by that proposition. 'But we…*can't*—'

Nik rested a silencing fingertip against her parted lips. 'Right at this moment the only thing that matters is that you get stronger and healthier. You don't have to make *any* big permanent decisions while we're here,' he assured her with determined emphasis.

Her eyes opened very wide. 'Sex *isn't* a big decision?'

In answer, Nik flashed her a wickedly amused grin. It filled his lean, darkly beautiful features with such charisma that the roof could've fallen in without her noticing. 'Not when we're married and you're already pregnant. What is the worst that could happen now?' he drawled silkily. 'That you might enjoy yourself?'

The warmth in her cheeks increased and she tore her gaze from his in self-protection, ashamed of her susceptibility. She had always enjoyed herself with him in bed. From the very first time to the very last time, sex with Nik had been a guaranteed passport to a wickedly seductive world of euphoric physical sensation. Long brown fingers gently circled her ankle and smoothed along the bare skin of her calf. A little tremor ran through her slight body and her lashes shot up again to focus on his lean, hard-boned face. In self-defence she closed her eyes but the predatory blaze of explosive hunger that had greeted her in his intense gaze was seared on the inside of her eyelids. *Nik wanted her every bit as much as she wanted him.* The awareness soothed her stinging pride but did nothing to assuage the flickers of eager warmth tingling through her lower body.

'Allow me…' Nik bent over her to run down the side zip on her dress and then without hesitation he gathered up the hem and lifted the garment off over her head.

'What are you doing?' Betsy whipped defensive hands over her bared breasts as they spilled free of the supportive bodice.

'Tucking you in.' Nik slid a hand below her hips to ease her free of the bedding, flipped it back and settled her down on the cool sheet. 'Drop the modesty. Let me enjoy the view.'

Her heart beating very fast, Betsy lowered her hands, feeling a little foolish for that belated cover-up. After all, they were married. And he had already told her that they could have sex without him assuming that it meant they were reconciled. Could she take that cool, sensible stance too? Her every emotion battled against such a concept. But at the same time there was no way she was ready yet to give him a final answer on whether or not she believed they could rebuild their marriage.

'There's more of you now to appreciate and you were already beautiful, *yineka mou,*' Nik husked, appraising the fuller contours of her small breasts before lowering his dark head to lick the lush, prominent peak of a swollen pink nipple while his fingers delicately shaped the new ripeness of her flesh. 'This, however, is for your pleasure, not mine. I want you to relax.'

Her breath hitched in her dry throat and she slumped back against the pillows, weak with longing and more than willing to let him play with her treacherous body but very far from being in a relaxed state. He dallied with the straining buds, utilising every ounce of skill in his armoury to tease her sensitised flesh. Heat thrummed to another level between her slender, trembling thighs, while her hips shifted back and forth in a movement she couldn't control. He tugged off her panties and leant back to slowly run his hands up the full length of her extended legs and ease them apart. Eyes hot on hers, he vented an appreciative masculine growl when his fingertips came into contact with the honeyed moisture coating her hidden core.

He drew her back into the hard heat of his taut, muscular body, covering her mouth with his. His tongue delved and explored and desire burned higher in Betsy than a firework shooting into the sky. Her hands clutched at his shoulders before lacing into his luxuriant black hair to hold him fast. He was a very sexy kisser. While he engaged her lips his hands roved until, freeing her mouth, he pulled her back against him and gently, softly, touched her between her trembling thighs.

Between one heartbeat and the next, her whole body became a mass of screaming nerve endings and she quivered and shook in response against him, her breath releasing in muffled sobs and gasps. Against her hip she could feel him hard and ready even through the barrier of his trousers. 'Make love to me,' she urged helplessly.

'Later,' Nik husked, burying his mouth against her exposed throat and licking and nipping at the sensitive cords of muscle pulling taut there to send another wave of painfully erotic stimulation through her already tormented body. 'Come for me...'

His stubbled jawline rasped against her cheek as he touched her with aching expertise and suddenly there was nothing she could do about it, her body was racing for the finish line all on its own. A liquid flame ran through her as unstoppable as a tide and the tightness in her pelvis suddenly clenched and convulsed in an explosion of almost intolerable pleasure as spasm after spasm of ecstatic release gripped her.

Nik settled her limp length back against the pillows. 'Now you sleep,' he rasped.

Betsy's face felt hot enough to fry eggs on and she didn't open her eyes as he tugged the cool linen sheet over her hot, damp body. She was limp with shame at having succumbed to temptation and taken the pleasure he offered. Once again she had stomped all over her own most deeply held principles. But then hadn't she always done that to keep Nik in her life? She had married a man who did not love her and from that moment on *everything* had become a compromise. In the same way, if they reconciled to raise their unborn children, she would never have the security of knowing herself loved and would have to live with the truth that only her fertility had brought him back to her.

And that was a toxic truth, she acknowledged painfully, one that would twist and grow inside her like Jack's beanstalk and eventually smother her self-esteem. But if the only alternative was to stay separated and continue the divorce, would that be any easier? After all, with her being pregnant they could not have a clean break now. Could she live with Nik always on the periphery of her life as the father of her children? Look on with detachment when he eventually chose another woman to share his life?

Pain slammed through her in answer to that question. Her lashes lifted as she stole an anguished glance at his bold bronzed profile, insecurity clawing at her.

For a split second she wanted his arms round her so badly it hurt. *Later,* she recalled, a little bubble of heat warming her chilled limbs at the promise of that word. And in the back of her mind, she cringed at what loving Nik had done to her pride. Would she only feel secure now when he demonstrated desire for her body?

CHAPTER EIGHT

OVER BREAKFAST ON the sunlit terrace the following morning, Betsy studied Nik's lean bronzed face with its sleek yet hard-edged charisma, feminine appreciation sending prickles of awareness slivering through her pelvis. At the same time she was wondering why he hadn't joined her in bed the previous night. She assumed it was because her long and very sound sleep had convinced him that her need for rest was more important.

'So, what would you like to do today?' Nik enquired lazily.

'Obviously I want to see where you grew up…in fact every place on this island that's associated with your childhood!' Betsy confessed with helpless enthusiasm.

Seriously taken aback by that chirpy admission, Nik briefly froze. A split second later he concealed his reaction by forcing a transient smile to his lips while he scanned Betsy's happy and relaxed expression. No, she had not the slightest suspicion that she had dropped a brick. And Vesos was, after all, where he had grown up. Her expectation that, having brought her here, he would want to share childhood experiences was simply normal. Acknowledging that truth, Nik cursed his decision to come to the island in the first place. Why hadn't he just hired a villa some-where? Vesos and this house had seemed the most sensible choice when they were already in Greece. But it had also been the very *last* place he had wanted to revisit, he reflected grudgingly.

Rising with something less than his usual grace from his seat, Nik stood gazing out through the trees towards the sea, mastering the powerful emotions threatening to roar through him like a hurricane, his broad back and wide shoulders rigid with tension. My mistake, he conceded heavily, and what could he do but play along to satisfy her natural curiosity? And why not when he was an adult now and no longer a weak and frightened child? Betsy wanted pretty, cosy pictures and he would give her pretty, cosy pictures, not the awful, pity-inducing truth.

'You started school here?' Betsy prompted over an hour later as she studied the small brick-built build-ing beside the harbour and the young children play-ing outside with fascination.

Nik nodded and barely repressed a shudder. He thought of the bruising a teacher had once questioned and the lies he had been forced to tell to hide the re-ality of what went on within his own home. School had been difficult, not, of course, in academic terms but in the pain of the gradual dawning realisation that other children did not appear to suffer the treatment that he did. It had been a challenge for him to make friends, set apart as he was by his family's wealth, even more of a challenge to play when he didn't know *how* to play.

'I really wish we could go and see your grandfather's house—' Betsy admitted.

No, no, no, *no,* Nik reflected sickly, nausea stirring at such a disturbing prospect.

'But I know it's your mother's house now,' Betsy allowed ruefully. 'Couldn't we drive past it?'

Nik was willing to settle for that less menacing suggestion. He drove along the coast road towards the cliffs.

'Did you play on this beach?'

'I was never allowed to leave the grounds of my grandfather's home unless I had an adult with me,' Nik fielded wryly, struggling to think of some single sunny recollection of his earliest years that would satisfy her desire to know more, but coming up with nothing.

Betsy peered at the house through the tall wrought-iron electric gates while Nik stared out through the windscreen without turning his dark head, lean brown hands flexing round the steering wheel of the sports car. 'It's an enormous place,' she commented, glancing at him, wondering why he was so quiet and *so...* She struggled and failed to come up with an adequate label for his attitude. 'Which bit of it did you live in?'

'The wing furthest away from the gate,' Nik related flatly. 'It was entirely self-contained—my mother insisted on having her privacy.'

'Were you happy here?' Betsy prompted gently.

'Of course I was,' Nik lied.

'So, when are we leaving?' Betsy asked casually over dinner almost a week later.

Nik frowned and studied her with questioning green eyes clear as emeralds ringed by spiky black lashes. 'Why would we be leaving?'

It was Betsy's turn to be disconcerted. 'Because we have to be back for Belle's birthday party on Friday night,' she pointed out.

'I don't see why,' Nik countered, cradling his wine lazily in one lean, elegant hand. 'We'll send her a special present instead—'

Betsy stiffened. 'No. I want to attend her party. I always assumed we'd be returning in time for it.'

Nik shrugged a broad shoulder while studying her with quiet satisfaction. Even in the short time they had spent on the island Betsy had blossomed. Her skin had acquired a light golden tint and her eyes were no longer shadowed. Her face was fuller, softer, the previous tension etched there banished by a regime of good food, afternoon naps and regular swimming sessions. When the local doctor had checked her blood pressure the day before, the reading had been normal and Nik believed that his decision to stay on Vesos had been fully vindicated. Here on the island, Betsy had nothing to do but get out of bed in the morning. Rest and relaxation had proved to be all she truly needed to regain her strength.

'It never occurred to me that you would want to attend Belle's party,' he admitted levelly. 'You're doing so well here. I think we should stay on for at least another week.'

Betsy had stiffened defensively. 'No, I can't do that—'

'Of course you can,' Nik told her in a 'subject closed' tone of voice lightly tinged with impatience and dismissal. 'Belle will understand that your health must come first—'

'For goodness' sake, there's nothing wrong with me any more!' Betsy argued, planting her hands firmly to the table and pushing herself upright as she thrust her chair back. 'I'm feeling a lot better and you know it!'

Nik uncoiled his long, lean length from the seat opposite with a positively slothful grace that mocked her angry, impatient movements. 'I don't understand why you're getting so annoyed—'

'Of course you don't. You're too accustomed to me doing everything you ask!' Betsy condemned, angry with him, angry with herself, for hadn't she taken the path of least resistance too often in recent days? For almost a week she had been painfully sensible and she had followed all Mr Xenophon's advice while at the same time taking on board Nik's suggestions. 'But I'm not going to go on acting like a doormat!'

His lean dark features hardened. 'I have not treated you like a doormat—'

'That's what I used to behave like and how you're used to dealing with me,' Betsy reasoned bitterly. 'But I'm not the same woman I was before you started the divorce, so laying down the law, giving me your opinion and making it clear what *you* want isn't going to make me change my mind about what *I* want to do!'

Nik ignored that direct challenge and said instead, 'Why is this party so important to you?'

'Because it's important to Belle and she and Cristo are family, not to mention my best friends…or haven't you realised that?' Betsy prompted, happily leaping off on another tangent because even before he had spoken she had not been in the best of moods. 'Who do you think supported me when the divorce started? Your brother! Cristo was really, *really* good to me—'

Nik chose not to mention that he had encouraged that connection but he was taken aback by her vehemence. 'Don't think I'm not grateful for that—'

'Like you cared at the time!' Betsy slung back at him in furious rebuttal. 'Cristo *listened* to me, talked to me, helped me through the worst period of my life. And Belle was generous enough to offer me her friendship from the very beginning—'

'Well, she never offered it to me,' Nik responded drily.

'Belle resents the fact that you've never shown the smallest interest in her mother and your father's children!'

'I never knew Gaetano. Why would his other children interest me? It's different with Cristo—he's an adult and we have a genuine bond—'

'Well, just you remember that those same children are going to be our babies' uncles and aunts!' Betsy reminded him tartly. 'Let's hope they feel friendlier towards our children in the future than you are to them.'

Lean dark features clenching hard, Nik gazed steadily back at her and slowly compressed his sculpted lips. 'I hadn't thought of that aspect. It does put a different complexion on the situation.'

Disconcerted by that concession though she was, Betsy made no comment. Instead she said, 'Why are you always so negative about Gaetano Ravelli?'

'Why wouldn't I be? As a father, he was an embarrassment. He lived off women like a gigolo—'

'But he was married to your mother, Cristo's mother and Zarif's,' she contradicted in surprise at his opinion.

'Surely you must have appreciated that Gaetano only ever married rich women for what he could get out of them? He got no money from my mother solely because their beach wedding in South America wasn't legal,' Nik advanced with derision. 'Helena deliberately neglected to file the right documents because she already suspected Gaetano of infidelity with Cristo's mother. Once she had the proof of it, she got rid of him and he couldn't claim a penny from her. How can you expect me to have any respect for a man that calculating and greedy?'

'Well, hopefully Gaetano's children by Belle's mother will grow up into decent people. You shouldn't hold their parentage against them. After all, you don't hold it against Cristo or Zarif,' she reminded him.

His mobile phone rang and she walked away, leaving him to answer it, and went out to the terrace.

There she perched on a low wall to listen to the distant sound of the surf washing the shore beyond the trees while striving to breathe in deep and let her bad mood simply evaporate.

His unbuttoned shirt blowing back in the breeze, Nik strolled along the terrace talking on the phone in measured Greek. His strong shoulder muscles bunched and kicked back as he gave a languorous stretch, arching his long spine so that his washboard abs pulled tight into mouth-watering definition. Betsy couldn't take her eyes off his spectacular body or the downy little furrow of hair that swam into view above his shorts as he breathed in, chest swelling, stomach tightening, causing the waistband to drop even lower on his lean brown hips. Heat flooded her face and her body and, half angry, half amused at her own behaviour, she tore her gaze from him and stared out into the darkness instead.

Considering that 'later' had never come around a week ago, looking was the only sensual pleasure she had, Betsy reflected, tensing at the thought and the feelings of hurt and rejection it evoked. For some reason, Nik had backed away from the idea of intimacy. Not only did he cart her up and downstairs with the detachment of a block of wood but he had also chosen to sleep in the bedroom next door. His retreat on that front had taken Betsy by surprise because Nik had always been very highly sexed. Even worse from her point of view, her body was awash with hormones and raring to go with an enthusiasm she had never experienced before.

She remembered that sexy little interlude on the evening of their arrival and breathed in deep and slow to cool her rising temperature. What had changed for Nik since that night? Did the very fact that she was pregnant make her less attractive on his terms? She supposed that was perfectly possible, particularly to a male who had never wanted children. Now that children were on the way, Nik might be ready to take responsibility as a parent but who was to say how he *really* felt about the development? A man wasn't committed simply because he said and did the right things. It was even possible that her less than enthusiastic reaction to the offer of reconciliation had annoyed and offended him. Nik was a proud man. He had tried to build a bridge between them and she was still standing frozen in the middle of that bridge, moving neither forward nor back, paralysed by indecision and terrified of doing the wrong thing.

Yet he had given her every opportunity to discuss her insecurities. Only, when had deep, meaningful conversations *ever* worked with Nik? When he didn't talk back it was a waste of her breath and when he brooded in silence she felt even worse. And when, as now, he might feel that for the sake of her health and peace of mind he had to tell her whatever she wanted to hear, how likely was it that he would feel that he could be honest? Throughout the week, Nik had displayed endless concern about her well-being. Fortunately her appetite had returned and she was sleeping soundly again, pleasantly tired after daily swimming sessions and walks on the beach. But the emergency, such as it had been, was over now and he needed to accept that and stop treating her like an invalid.

Tossing his phone down on the table, Nik came to a sudden halt in front of her. His wide, sensual mouth compressed. 'Look, if Belle's party is *that* important to you, we'll leave tomorrow,' he delivered grimly. 'But I don't agree with it—'

Surprise and pleasure darted through Betsy that he had given way. He might not understand the depth of her friendship with Cristo and Belle but he was trying to respect it. Without thinking about it, she stretched up on tiptoe to link her arms round his neck. 'You'll enjoy seeing Cristo, and Belle told me that Zarif is trying to clear his schedule to attend as well…'

The warmth of her smile lit up her heart-shaped face. It was relatively easy to make Betsy happy; Nik had realised that a long time ago but he had fallen out of the habit. But then in the early days he had had to negotiate a welter of misapprehensions before he had found the right path. It was not the cost of the gift that mattered but the thought and the effort behind it. It could be as simple as making a phone call, regardless of how busy he was, or of sharing the minutiae of his busy day to make her feel a part of it. Back then an unexpectedly sunny morning, the random kindness of a stranger or a casual compliment could leave Betsy wreathed in smiles.

'Oh, joy, my brother the king with the big mouth,' Nik derided as he looked down at her and slowly closed his arms round her slight body.

Betsy groaned out loud, having forgotten that complication. 'I think Zarif did you a favour, so cut him some slack. I had to find out about the vasectomy at some stage,' she pointed out ruefully. 'You had backed yourself into a corner by not telling me about it and I don't think you knew how to get out of it.'

Nik was genuinely stunned by that shrewd assessment of his behaviour. Ebony lashes shielded his reflective gaze but his thoughts were short-circuited by the soft, full mouth pressing to the corner of his with unstudied warmth. Betsy smelled of peaches and vanilla, and every barrier he had raised against temptation was washed away as if a tidal wave had engulfed him. His hands slid down to her delicately curved hips and he hoisted her up against him and brought his mouth crashing down on hers with hungry enthusiasm.

'Why did I have to wait so long for that?' Betsy moaned helplessly, struggling to relocate her breath while every skin cell in her body erupted into sudden life.

Nik stiffened defensively at the question and then set her circumspectly down again. 'Because if I can't finish, I don't want to start,' he told her frankly.

Brow furrowing, Betsy stared up at him. 'Why can't you finish?'

Nik groaned. 'You're supposed to be resting, taking it easy—'

Betsy flushed. 'But Mr Xenophon told me that making love would be OK.'

Nik froze in surprise. 'And when did he tell you that?'

'While I was getting dressed and you were in his office, because that's when I asked him what I should be avoiding—'

'*Diavelos!* Why didn't you tell me?' Nik suddenly demanded, studying her in disbelief.

'Well, the first night here, you seemed perfectly comfortable—'

'And then I came downstairs while you slept...' Nik exclaimed, stretching out his arms in emphasis. 'And I thought, what the hell am I doing here? Why am I assuming that a pregnant woman is in any fit state for a sexual marathon? That has to be the very *last* thing she needs in her current state of health!'

Betsy blinked, putting the facts together, amazed that she had been as foolish in her own way as he had been. He had assumed he should keep his distance and she had assumed that he simply didn't want her enough. 'We don't talk enough,' she murmured ruefully.

'And we're not going to talk very much tonight or indeed for the remainder of our stay,' Nik forecast, a breathtaking smile of intent slashing his beautiful stubborn mouth as he scooped her up into his arms and headed straight for the stairs. 'I have other plans.'

'Extensive, I hope,' Betsy encouraged, turquoise eyes locked to his lean, darkly handsome face, true energy leaping through her for the first time in days because the desire he couldn't hide in his possessive gaze restored her battered self-esteem.

'*Very* extensive,' Nik promised, laying her down on her bed, pulling off her shoes, flipping her over to unzip her dress and flipping her back to trail her out of its concealing folds to leave her exposed in a lacy bra and panties set. 'You look amazing—'

Betsy shifted uneasily. 'No, I don't... I'm losing my waist—'

'You *do* look amazing. I don't say anything I don't mean.' Nik shrugged off his shirt, loosed the button at the waist of his shorts. 'I've hardly slept this week. It's been so hot and the nights are very long when you have a hard-on that won't quit...'

Betsy watched his spectacular lean bronzed length emerge as the garments slid away. Her heartbeat was racing. He was fully erect and ready for action and her self-consciousness ebbed as though he had thrown a switch inside her. She sat up, unclasped her bra and skimmed off her panties with an eagerness she had never really dared to show him before. A predatory grin of appreciation slashing his mouth as she unveiled her succulent breasts, Nik came down on his knees on the bed.

'Multiply amazing by ten,' he advised, brushing his mouth across a straining pink nipple.

'You're just sex-starved—'

'Totally,' Nik agreed without shame. 'I haven't had sex since I got you pregnant...'

'Or after leaving me,' she reminded him, stroking an appreciative hand down the velvety length of his boldly aroused shaft in a way that made him jerk and suppress a moan.

Nik lounged back against the tumbled white pillows, the very image of sleek, dark, sexy masculinity.

Blue eyes bright with hunger, Betsy bent over him. Silky blonde hair fanned his abdomen and brushed his lean, hair-roughened thighs, and his breath caught on a groan of pleasure. He wanted her so much. He had never ever wanted anything so much.

'Enough,' he urged hoarsely, tugging a strand of pale hair to restrain her. 'Words can't describe the pleasure of what you're doing to me but I want to come inside you.'

Heat was already throbbing between her thighs and she could feel the moisture gathering there. He tugged her up into his arms and fastened his mouth to a lush rosy nipple, lashing the prominent bud with his tongue, and her spine arched and her pelvis brushed against his arousal. She came down with her knees either side of him and instinctively glided the neediest part of her back and forth over him.

'Hot,' Nik pronounced appreciatively, green eyes glittering like jewels in his lean, strong face. 'Am I allowed to assume that you've found the nights long and unsatisfying too?'

'You are,' Betsy confided, quivering over him, alight with so many different sensations she was intoxicated by that physical contact.

He took her mouth, his tongue plunging deep, his hand knotted in her hair to hold her fast. His dominance excited her beyond bearing. His other hand was engaged in darting explorations of whichever part of her was within reach and she immediately shifted up higher on him, squashing her tingling breasts against the hard, solid wall of his chest, settling her hot, damp core down to ride astride a lean, powerful thigh, and attempted to rock away the tormenting ache of emptiness afflicting her.

'Be patient…we've got all night,' Nik growled urgently.

'To heck with patience!' Betsy almost sobbed against his wildly demanding mouth, her fingers biting into the satin-smooth width of his shoulders.

A disconcerted sound of amusement was wrenched from Nik. He reached for her and lifted her, rearranging her over him to realign their bodies. He angled up his lean hips, initially sliding against her before finding entry with a sudden precision that wrested a sob of wonder and pleasure from her parted lips.

'Never say I can't take a hint,' Nik teased breathlessly, settling her over him and driving deep and then finally, with a revealing sound of frustration, he eased her over and pinned her flat to the mattress under him. 'Better?'

He thrust into her hard and she felt every inch of him and the delicious friction of the movement sent tiny convulsive tremors rippling through her womb.

'Perfect,' she told him, barely able to find her voice.

And it was, absolutely perfect in every way. With every driving stroke of his possession he unleashed a storm of pleasure on her eager body. She lifted her hips and bucked beneath him, matching his insistent rhythm while the consuming, tormenting delight grew and soared to a blinding high of raw excitement. Her heart thumping like crazy in her ears, she flew higher than ever before, carried by the wild throbbing pleasure to a stormy climax that lit her up inside and out with joy and sweet release.

'So, Cinderella shall go to the ball,' Nik mused huskily into her damp, tumbled hair. 'In fact if this is your response to the chance of attending a family party, I will find a party for you every night.'

A choked giggle escaped Betsy. He rolled onto a cooler patch of the bed, taking her with him, draping her over his sprawled powerful length with careful hands, fingers smoothing down her slender spine. It was a long time since anything had felt so right to her as the peace she experienced in the protective circle of his arms. She was tempted to tell him that she loved him but she swallowed the words that she had once offered so freely and with such trust, impervious to the reality that he did not return those words. She was not so naïve now. She rubbed her chin against a broad bronzed shoulder and drank in the hot, musky scent of him like an addict, happy, content but frightened that she was being foolish and short-sighted about the future.

Could she dare to trust Nik Christakis again? Could he be persuaded to make more of an effort this time around? Perhaps she should negotiate with him before she agreed to a proper reconciliation. Sometimes she thought Nik understood business deals much better than he did human relationships. If she laid out her needs as terms and conditions, would he listen then? What could she offer him in return? That second chance he had mentioned and as much sex as he could handle? Hot-faced, she grinned against his shoulder, struggling to pin her dizzy feet to planet earth again and be sensible. She had to learn to be as logical as Nik was and address future problems in a positive rather than critical way.

CHAPTER NINE

NIK STUDIED BETSY as if she had gone insane without him having noticed, with wonder and disbelief and, yes, unfortunately, just a little amusement. 'Let me get this straight…you want to negotiate the terms of our marriage *before* you'll consider making a reconciliation permanent?'

In the background the hum of the jet engines provided a surprisingly soothing backdrop to Betsy's ears. Nik was a trapped audience when he was airborne. He couldn't walk away, make an excuse about pressing business or lose his temper because he would dislike the risk of the cabin crew overhearing him arguing with his wife.

'Yes. I think it's the practical approach. We failed the first time around, so we should try to foresee the potential problems there might be and endeavour to avoid them this time,' Betsy responded doggedly, lifting her chin as Nik sprang restively out of his seat and frowned down at her.

'But we didn't *have* any problems the first time— you decided you wanted a baby, I knew I couldn't

give you one and it all went downhill from there,'
Nik recited drily.

'It only went downhill because *you* decided that
you couldn't tell me the truth about your vasectomy,'
Betsy contradicted.

His green eyes glittered with challenge and his
strong jawline clenched hard with tension. 'How
many men want to tell a woman that they can't give
her the one thing she most wants in the world?' he
demanded in a harsh undertone. 'How do you think
I felt when I stumbled on the baby clothes you had
hidden in a bag at the back of the closet?'

Betsy was taken aback by that bold and unusually
emotional question. It made her appreciate for the
first time that Nik's macho spirit had been crucified
by her desire for what he had known he could not
give her; she had made him feel inadequate. When
he mentioned the secret cache of baby items she had
bought as a gesture of continuing hope and then
shamefacedly hidden, she didn't know where to put
herself. She was deeply embarrassed by that revelation, did not even want to think about how that discovery must have made him feel, and her face burned
with discomfiture.

'I didn't know you'd found those clothes… Why
didn't you tell me?' she pressed weakly.

'I knew I was in way over my head, so it was easier
and safer to avoid the subject,' Nik admitted grimly.
'There was no way out for me that I could see. As far
as I knew then the vasectomy was irreversible and no

matter what I did you were going to break your heart for what I could *never* hope to give you...'

'I'm so sorry,' Betsy whispered feelingly, finally recognising what that troubled phase of their lives had cost him as well. Her desire for a child had become an obsession that had ruled her existence *and* his and he had been trapped by a truth that he could not bear to share with her.

But now everything had changed, she reminded herself impatiently. Against all the odds, she had conceived that much-wanted baby and what she was fighting for now was the need for them to create a viable blueprint for their marriage to thrive in the future.

'These terms you mentioned...' Nik prompted softly but she wasn't fooled by his tone. He stood straight and tall, lean, darkly beautiful face taut as if he was daring her to suggest conditions that he would find unacceptable.

'You were always travelling and I was home alone. That would have to change,' Betsy told him ruefully.

Nik viewed her in astonishment. 'But I wasn't away on pleasure trips. I was travelling for business reasons—'

'I know, but you were never at home and I got very lonely,' Betsy forced herself to admit with bald honesty. 'I was lucky to see you one week a month. It wasn't enough.'

Nik was sharply disconcerted. 'As a husband my most basic function is surely to be a good provider for you?'

'That would sound very impressive and I could

forgive your absences if your business was in trouble or you weren't already richer than Croesus. But you don't have either excuse. Ideally, I want a husband who thinks that his most basic function should be to make me happy,' Betsy confided valiantly. 'And it would make me much happier if you were at home more, particularly once the children are born. You need to be on the spot to be a good father.'

Nik was broodingly silent. It had never occurred to him that she could be lonely when he wasn't around. After all, in the first years of their marriage she had never once complained about the amount of time they spent apart. It was true that she had once said that loneliness had initially led to her desire for a child, but he had assumed that that was a momentary source of unhappy frustration, more of an excuse on her part than an actual fault that could be laid at his door.

'A long time ago, my grandfather taught me that the only person you can really trust in business is yourself and you're asking me to delegate important functions to subordinates,' he informed her heavily. 'I don't know if I can do that...'

He was so serious, so very serious. She had asked him to travel less, stay home more, but the way he was reacting she might as well have asked him to give her a daily pint of his blood or sacrifice a limb. Her hands knotted by her sides to prevent her from reaching out to him because until that moment she had never appreciated just how deep his distrust of others went or that that distrust had been fostered in him at an early age by a close relative.

'But you could *try*,' she pointed out gently. 'Try and see how it goes because if you don't try another way of living I can't see how I'll ever be happy with you.'

Nik was taken aback by that underwritten threat. He knew men who would be grateful to learn that their wives wanted to see more of them. He knew even more how grateful he had always been to come home to Betsy, even during the baby-obsessed phase of their marriage. Then, quick as a flash, another acknowledgement gripped him. In a few months' time they would have two young children in their lives and that fast and that easily Nik understood where his first priority should lie. He could not protect children whom he rarely saw. He could not be a good father or a good husband without making compromises. But, as always, when sudden change threatened, Nik froze, filled with sudden dread and disquiet at the prospect of his careful routine being disrupted.

'What's wrong?' Betsy queried.

'Nothing,' Nik declared instantly, veiling his gaze and breathing in slow and deep in a control exercise he had been taught to utilise at the tender age of ten. No child of his would ever be similarly afflicted. The knowledge that he would do everything possible to protect his children soothed him.

Betsy moved forward, painfully aware that Nik was locked in an intense introspection that took hold of him occasionally and shut her out. She ran her palms up over his shirtfront, exulting in the heat and hard strength of him, wishing he would share what was troubling him. 'You and I…it can work,' she told him steadily. 'We can *make* it work.'

His lean, powerful length tensing for a different reason as his body's natural instincts took over from his brain, Nik stared down into anxious azure eyes and a hundred memories threatened to entrap him: Betsy struggling to hide her difficulty in reading the menu at their first dinner date; Betsy laughing in the rain when her umbrella broke and she got soaked; Betsy teaching Gizmo to return a ball rather than chewing it to pieces; Betsy telling him he had got her pregnant. She was both fearless and frank with that take-it-or-leave-it honesty that he had always cherished. It was a shame he couldn't match that honesty, couldn't tell her what had happened to him, but he believed that the truth would only weaken him in her eyes and ultimately frighten her and she depended on him to protect her. He was caught between a rock and a hard place.

'Betsy…' he husked not quite evenly, fingers lacing into her silky blonde hair to brush it back from her cheekbone.

'We can make each other happy. We can make it work,' she repeated with dogged conviction.

'Shut up,' he told her in Greek and he kissed her with urgent claiming force.

It was a kiss filled with lust and frustration and it was hotter than the fires of hell, burning through Betsy like a flaming arrow that ignited a wanton ache between her slender thighs. She fell into that kiss like a falling star and burned up. When he gathered her up in his arms and carried her through to the sleeping compartment, she looked up at him with her heart in her eyes, warmth and fear and longing all tangled up together, but she still didn't give him the words of love she had once given so trustingly. Once she said those words, she couldn't take them back again, couldn't impose any distance between them and couldn't make the same demands. Once she said them he would know her for a fake; he would know she wouldn't turn her back or walk away. Not because she didn't want to but because she simply *couldn't*...

CHAPTER TEN

BETSY GRIMACED AT her reflection in the mirror. She was getting ready for Belle's party but her thoughts were far removed from frivolity.

If Nik had loved her, she was convinced she could have buried every atom of her insecurity for ever. As it was, unhappily, she was convinced that her husband had only returned to her because she was pregnant and that knowledge was a humiliation that would only fester with every passing year. Her troubled blue eyes dampened. Blinking ferociously fast, she quickly grabbed up a tissue to soak up the tears before she could smudge her mascara.

But it was a fact that Nik didn't love her and never had loved her. He lusted after her like crazy, a chemical connection that had evidently kept him true even while they were separated. Be grateful for what you have rather than yearning for what you can't have, Betsy urged herself in frustration. After all, some people would kill for the power to ignite such high-voltage passion in a partner. It should be enough. It *had* to be enough.

It was barely twenty-four hours since they had returned to Lavender Hall and a good deal of that time they had spent in bed. Her face burned at the recollection. She couldn't stop wanting Nik, couldn't put the brakes on the wild, greedy hunger he invoked every time she looked at him. But if she continued to be so easily available, how long would it be before Nik recognised that he had her exactly where he wanted her? In the palm of his hand to treat as he saw fit. A position of such weakness and vulnerability could never be a good starting point, particularly for a shiny new reconciliation.

Pale blonde hair, freshly washed and dried, swung in a silken bell round her shoulders as she walked back into the bedroom. Almost simultaneously, Nik strode out of the dressing room, fully dressed and immaculate. In a designer jacket teamed with close-fitting black trousers that enhanced his height, narrow hips and long, muscular legs, he looked absolutely gorgeous, all dark and sleek and the very ultimate in raw sexual power.

Heat pooled low in Betsy's pelvis and she fought that sizzle of awareness with every fibre she possessed. After all, there was no point trying to play it cool with Nik to keep him on his metaphoric toes while at the same time falling into the nearest bed with him at every possible opportunity. Wasn't that what she had been doing? Whenever she looked at Nik, she could barely keep her hands off him.

Nik studied her with unconcealed appreciation. 'Blue is definitely your colour, *kardoula mou*.'

Betsy's midnight-blue evening dress was fitted at breast and hip and the sleeves and skirt were made of lace. Her pale skin gleamed with the shimmer of a pearl through the mesh and her bright eyes reflected that rich blue like a mirror.

'I appreciate you coming to this with me. I know you don't like parties unless you're tucked away somewhere quiet talking solely about business,' Betsy remarked ruefully. 'But you'll have your brothers there for company—'

'And all the little half-brothers and sisters,' Nik reminded her wryly. 'I'll make an effort to get to know them but, as I lack small talk and Belle's probably already given them a poor impression of me, I can't make any promises.'

'A little bit of an effort is all that is required from you,' Betsy assured him, trying not to smile at his willingness to extend an olive branch to Gaetano Ravelli's youngest children. He had listened to her and he was prepared to change the status quo and to her way of thinking that was more than enough to earn him four gold stars.

'Obviously I'm willing to make any effort required,' Nik countered.

Betsy looked up at him with her very blue eyes. 'Why?'

Nik linked his arms round her still-slim waist, slowly easing her slender body into connection with his while he stared down at her with green eyes that had flared to jewelled brilliance with desire. 'I want you to be happy with me, Betsy.'

'I *am* happy,' she assured him, colour rising in her cheeks, hugely erotically aware of his big, powerful body and the erection he was making no attempt to hide. She stared up at him, treacherously enthralled by his sleek, dark, masculine beauty. The knowledge that in every way that mattered he was still hers in spite of the separation they had endured thrilled her and played merry havoc with her defences. Her body hummed at her feminine core, desire stirring in her, even while common sense fought to suppress it and remind her that she was all dressed up and keen to arrive on time for the party.

Nik lowered his handsome dark head and in an abrupt motion Betsy twisted her head aside, fighting her natural inclinations before he could succeed and wreck her lipstick. 'I'm all done up now,' she reasoned in breathless excuse and then glanced up at him, disconcerted when she recognised a fleeting flash of wounded uncertainty in his gaze. Her heart leapt in dismay at the memory that look provoked. He had looked at her precisely like that the day he had walked out, as if he didn't understand quite what he had done by making a secret of his vasectomy, couldn't credit her reaction to the revelation and was incredibly hurt by it. She hadn't understood it then but it still wasn't an expression she could be comfortable seeing him wear again.

In an equally sudden movement she pulled free of his arms and spun to present him with her back. 'Unzip me,' she instructed.

'But I *thought*—' he began in apparent mystification at her change of heart.

'Since when was I so fussy?' Betsy teased shakily, eyes over-bright with sudden tears, her pregnancy hormones all on override because she wanted him, she *always* wanted him and she marvelled that he should not immediately grasp that little fact.

The dress shimmered down to the floor and she stood revealed in lacy underwear. He feasted his eyes on her tiny, increasingly curvy body while she scooped up the gown and laid it carefully over a chair. 'Sometimes I want you so much it almost hurts,' he told her in a hoarse undertone.

Colour mounted in her cheeks as he shed his jacket and shirt with none of the care she had employed. She strolled back to him and unfastened his trousers, slender hands delving beneath to find the long, hard evidence of his arousal and stroke his velvet-smooth, rigid shaft with wondering fingers until he swore in guttural Greek under his breath and wrenched off the remainder of his clothing with less patience than he had shown a moment earlier. She knelt at his feet pleasuring him with her lush mouth and knowing fingers, excitement lancing almost painful waves of arousal through her heated body with every groan she wrenched from him.

'I want to make love to you,' Nik growled, bending down to scoop her up and plant her down squarely on the end of the bed. He skimmed off her knickers and ran the tip of his tongue across the pointed evidence of her achingly sensitive swollen nipples before test-

ing the honeyed welcome between her thighs with the
single dip of a long, appreciative finger.

Even before he came down over her, Betsy was
gasping and arching, unbearably eager for the finale
she longed for. Nik tipped her legs over his shoulders
and sank into her slick channel hard and fast, stretching her with delicious force.

'You're incredible in bed, *kardoula mou,*' he told
her rawly, angling back his hips before thrusting back
deep inside again in a movement that wrenched a
helpless cry from her convulsed throat.

Her heart raced and she struggled to breathe as the
excitement built, backed by the ever-tightening constraint of tension gripping her pelvis. His fast, fluid
rhythm became rougher, rawer as he pounded into her
and finally she lost control, overwhelmed by the passion and the wild explosion of pleasure that assailed her
when she could hold it back no longer. Even afterwards
little tremors of delight continued to rock through her
in rippling waves while she buried her face in Nik's
damp shoulder and drank in the hot, musky scent of
the lean, powerful body pinning hers to the mattress.

'I think we'd better make a move if we want to
make the party before midnight.' Mocking light green
eyes rested on her dazed expression and he laughed
as awareness reclaimed her, dismay flashed across
her face and she shoved against his shoulders, scrambling to get up and reclaim her party finery.

'I was really chuffed to see Nik taking some time to
chat to Bruno about his art course,' Belle confided

as she urged Betsy into the conservatory at the rear of the vast and luxurious London town house she and Cristo lived in. It was two in the morning and most of the party guests had already taken their leave.

'Nik probably finds Bruno less intimidating than his sisters,' Betsy joked.

'I invited far too many people tonight. I haven't been able to get five minutes alone with you all evening,' Belle complained, waving her glass of champagne in an emphatic gesture of annoyance, which sent a quantity of the golden liquid spilling over the lip of the goblet and down the stem.

Betsy laughed because the birthday girl was definitely a little tipsy. 'It's your party. Naturally everyone here wanted to speak to you personally—'

'But you and Nik…it's *definitely* all back on again?' the lively redhead asked with a fascination she couldn't conceal. 'When Cristo first told me that Nik had moved back into the hall, I refused to believe it.'

Betsy resisted an urge to admit that she too had initially been incredulous about that development. But some things were better kept private. 'The divorce is off,' she confirmed. 'We're going to try again.'

Smooth brow furrowing, Belle studied her with keen curiosity. 'In spite of everything that's happened between you? Regardless of everything he's done?'

Betsy chose to respond to those thorny questions with honesty. 'Apart from the fact that Nik's not the only one of us to have made mistakes, I never stopped loving him. I thought I had but then once I was with him again, I realised I'd only been kidding myself.'

In receipt of that confession, Belle unexpectedly looked surprisingly thoughtful and then she sighed in grudging surrender to the argument. 'I think we've all been there at some stage,' she confided with unexpected feeling. 'When I thought Cristo was in love with you, I honestly thought I hated him because I was devastated and so unbelievably jealous.'

Betsy froze to the spot in disbelief and wondered if she had misheard the other woman. 'You thought that Cristo could be in love with *me?* For goodness' sake, *when?*'

'After we got married I discovered that he carried a photo of you in his wallet,' Belle admitted ruefully. 'Before that find I had assumed that you were only friends—'

'But we *were* only friends,' Betsy retorted with uncomfortable stress, wondering just how much alcohol Belle had imbibed that evening. 'There was never anything else, not even a minor flirtation between us—I swear it—'

Belle wrinkled her nose in embarrassed dismissal. '*Of course* I know that now but I didn't know that back then and Cristo had quite a job convincing me because, let's face it, you are beautiful and very feminine, Betsy, so obviously I could see your appeal. At the time I was so afraid that you were much more Cristo's type than I could ever be—'

At that instant Belle's rambling speech was interrupted by a sudden noise behind Betsy and a harsh bitten-off masculine exclamation. She spun in consternation, just in time to see Nik's tall, broad-shouldered figure swinging round in the doorway to fire back out into the corridor.

'Nik?' she called after him anxiously while she wondered how long he had been standing there waiting for her to notice his presence. 'Were you looking for me? Wait for me…'

'Oh, *hell!*' Belle gasped in undiluted horror. 'Nik must've heard what I told you about Cristo…'

The two women raced out of the conservatory to return to the party and reached the hall just as Nik grabbed his brother Cristo by the shoulder and punched him in the face. A split second later Nik had Cristo physically pinned to a wall, black fury and outrage etched in every flushed line of his lean, rigid features. 'My wife…you were in love with *my* wife?' Nik was growling with enraged incredulity.

Betsy realised that Nik had indeed overheard Belle's deeply damaging admission that she had once believed that Cristo was in love with Betsy and she gritted her teeth in frustration at the realisation, because it was not at all the sort of revelation that Nik was likely to take lying down or with a large forgiving pinch of salt. Nik was a proud and possessive man and even his close friendship with his brother would not excuse what Nik would regard as an unforgivable betrayal of trust. Even so, it was all a stupid storm in a teacup, Betsy thought in exasperation, reluctant to credit that Belle's suspicions could ever have had any foundation in fact.

'Calm down, Nik. Think this through,' Cristo was urging with admirable cool for a male who had blood running from the corner of his mouth. 'You've got this all wrong—'

'You had a photo of Betsy in your wallet?' Nik was roaring, apparently deaf to any plea for calm.

'It's not like it sounds,' Cristo protested.

'My *own* brother? I trusted you, *totally* trusted you around my wife and you deceived me!' Nik growled as if Cristo hadn't even spoken and with that embittered accusation he threw back his arm and hit Cristo again.

Cristo finally tore himself free of Nik's punishing hold and shot a string of words at his brother in fast, fluent Italian.

'For goodness' sake, someone stop them!' Betsy exclaimed in consternation as the two brothers began to exchange punches in earnest with both of them so well matched in powerful build and strength that there was no hope of a quick conclusion to the fight.

Belle darted across the hall to the main reception room, which still contained a handful of lingering guests, and called her brother-in-law Zarif out to join them.

Zarif appeared in the doorway. Tall and startlingly handsome with olive skin and very dark eyes, the young King of Vashir took in the situation at a glance and waded between his brothers, ducking a blow that would have sent him flying had he not been so agile. Mercifully that near miss of their sovereign was all it took to provoke Zarif's four accompanying guards into plunging straight into the fight to forcibly separate the battling siblings. An exchange of furious Italian and Greek followed but Zarif flung open the door of Cristo's study and said drily, 'We will discuss this in a more private setting.'

Betsy dealt the younger man an appreciative appraisal, grateful for his intervention. While Zarif was technically merely a kid brother, he had been raised as an Arab prince in a royal palace and, having trained as a soldier and seen actual combat, he had a habit of command and a mature and level-headed presence far beyond his years.

'Oh, my heaven, what have I done to this family?' Belle was whispering, distraught, dashing her auburn hair off her brow in a feverish gesture. 'I've caused so much trouble between the brothers. Cristo will never forgive me for opening my big mouth.'

'No matter how he felt, Nik shouldn't have just exploded like that and assumed the worst,' Betsy breathed ruefully. 'He should have talked it over with Cristo first.'

'Nik would *still* have hit him,' Belle opined without hesitation. 'Nik's very much the dark, jealous, passionate type.'

Somehow Betsy had never viewed her husband in that light before and her lashes fluttered in confusion.

'And Cristo explained to me once that Nik's not good with emotional things, which I suppose explains why you almost got all the way to the divorce court before it finally dawned on Nik that you're *still* the most important person in his world.'

'I wouldn't put it quite like that,' Betsy muttered uncomfortably, wishing that she could crash into

Cristo's study to find out exactly what was happening between the three brothers. It was the very first time that she had seen Nik lose his temper and his self-control to that extent and she was still in shock, her legs feeling a little wobbly at having been witness to the kind of violence she abhorred, even more particularly when it broke out between members of the same family. That welter of exchanged blows had torn apart the brothers' close relationship and she was distressed by that reality.

'Nik's absolutely crazy about you!' Belle protested. 'And Cristo says he always has been…from the first moment he saw you.'

A lump formed in Betsy's throat. Was it possible that Nik truly cared about her? That he could have been as misled as she had been about her own feelings? After all, hadn't she believed that she hated Nik for a while? Hadn't that been her way of coping without him? Her way of getting by and surviving life without him?

'Cristo is just going to kill me for this mess,' Belle muttered guiltily, tears sparkling in her lovely eyes. 'I don't always think before I speak. Deep down inside me, I never forgot that time when I believed Cristo might care more for you than for me—'

'I don't believe that could ever have been the case,' Betsy countered staunchly.

'Maybe I wanted to test you, see how you reacted,' Belle acknowledged shamefacedly.

'I've just never seen Cristo as fanciable.' Intercepting Belle's rather chagrined glance, Betsy smiled wryly. 'There's never been anyone but Nik for me.'

Her steps uncertain, Betsy approached the study door and knocked on it before opening it. From the threshold she peered in at the brothers, all three of whom were posed with varying degrees of strain and annoyance etched in their remarkably similar lean features. 'I think we should go home now,' she told Nik flatly.

'Good idea.' Nik crossed the room with a flash of his long, powerful legs.

'And when you get there, you should explain some things to Betsy,' Cristo urged ruefully.

'That kind of interference is not within our remit,' Zarif chimed in, his tone one of reproach at that offering of advice.

As he listened to his brothers a line of colour flared along Nik's high cheekbones and then receded, leaving him curiously pale and extremely tense. Lush black lashes dipped down over his bright eyes as he dropped a protective arm round Betsy's slim shoulders. 'Home,' he agreed with unconcealed relief.

'Did you apologise to Cristo?' Betsy prompted as the limousine drew away from the town house.

Nik flashed her a stunned glance. 'No, I did not. Why would I apologise?'

Betsy breathed in slow and deep. 'You attacked him—'

'He got what he deserved,' Nik countered with caustic bite. 'It may be a little late in the day that he's getting it but he did deserve it. You're my wife and I trusted him with you—'

'And he never once betrayed that trust,' Betsy declared, choosing to be tactful rather than point out that during that period of their lives Nik had turned his back on their marriage and left her alone to sink or swim. 'If it's true that he did develop some sort of silly crush on me, I had no suspicion of it because he never said or did anything around me that even suggested that.'

'*Never?*' Nik pressed, shooting her a troubled and still-unconvinced appraisal. 'And how did you feel about Cristo at the time? I had gone, the divorce had started and you were alone but for my brother's *supportive* visits.' He spoke the word 'supportive' with deeply derisive emphasis.

'I was grateful for his support and the fact that he was willing to listen to me rambling on,' Betsy admitted honestly. 'I had nobody else to talk to. He was your brother. Talking about you to Cristo didn't feel disloyal and I *knew* that anything I said wouldn't go any further.'

'I encouraged him to connect with you,' Nik confided grittily, his jawline clenching hard at the recollection. 'I had total trust in him. I should have known better—'

'You *encouraged* him to be my friend?' Betsy repeated in surprise. 'But why?'

Nik shifted uneasily in his corner of the back seat. 'I wanted to know that you were all right, that you had everything you needed—'

'But I wasn't all right,' Betsy responded in a small, tight voice of commendable restraint. 'How could I have been? You had refused to even discuss your vasectomy and why you'd had it done and then you simply walked out on our marriage.'

Nik frowned, clearly thinking that evaluation unjust. 'Because you told me to leave. You said you could never forgive me, never look at me again and that I had killed your love. You said our marriage was over,' he replied.

Betsy studied his lean, darkly handsome face, taken aback to have her words of many months earlier thrown back at her when she'd least expected to hear them. 'But that's just the sort of thing people say when they're angry and hurt and crazily confused—'

'Only you can't afford to say stuff like that to me because I took it all literally and I believed that you meant every word that you said,' Nik admitted in a raw undertone.

Her brow indented. 'We should have talked again more calmly back then.'

'There were issues I wasn't prepared to discuss with you,' Nik vented grittily. 'I'm useless at discussing emotional stuff. If I don't even know quite how *I* feel, how am I supposed to know what anyone else is feeling?'

Frustration and bitterness roughened his dark deep drawl and she turned her head away, dropping her eyes, wondering what he was talking about but reluctant to put pressure on him after the upsetting evening they had had. 'Have you made up with Cristo?' she asked baldly.

'Were… *Are* you attracted to him?' Nik asked abruptly, his eyes light and bright in the dimness of the car interior. 'Most women would prefer him to me. I'm darker, rougher round the edges, a lot less smooth.'

Betsy swallowed hard, astonished that Nik could still seem so insecure and marvelling that he was still shaken up by Belle's revelation to continue feeling suspicious. 'All I can tell you is that I met the two of you together the same day at the bistro and I never really noticed him. I mean, I realised that there was a guy with you and I eventually worked out that you were brothers, but Cristo might as well not have been there for all the interest he inspired in me,' she confided quietly. 'It was you I noticed, you I couldn't take my eyes off—'

'And…later?' Nik pressed, closing a lean brown hand round hers where she had braced it on the leather seat. 'How did you feel later after our marriage broke down?'

'That he was my only friend, for listening and not judging. For being there when I needed a shoulder. He was very good to me—'

'He said I was a rotten husband, that I didn't treat you properly and that he felt sorry for you,' Nik breathed harshly. 'Is it true? Did I treat you badly?'

'You just travelled a lot and you were very… detached. You never explained anything. But aside of the vasectomy you kept quiet about, I wouldn't have termed you a rotten husband,' Betsy said truthfully. 'I was happy with you most of the time—'

'But it should have been *all* of the time,' Nik fielded grimly. 'I let you down. But with the exception of your desire for a child, I really thought I was doing OK in the husband category. Unfortunately I'm not perfect, in fact I'm seriously flawed and I've done as much as I can to remedy that. But then you're not quite perfect either. When I realised that you suffered from dyslexia I felt so comfortable with you. At first it was a wildfire physical attraction I felt for you, but once I got to know you and realised that you had restrictions as well, you seemed so perfect for me...'

The limousine drew up outside the hall and for a split second Betsy simply sat there, fixedly staring at Nik. *You had restrictions as well* was still ringing in her ears with the last two words ringing the loudest. 'When you said you were seriously flawed, what did you mean...?'

The passenger door whipped open and crisp, cool night air flooded in. Nik retained her hand and tugged her out of the car to guide her up the steps. 'I owe you the truth,' he intoned with a bitterness he couldn't hide. 'But it's a truth I would never have chosen to share with you.'

A chill of foreboding was sliding down Betsy's taut spinal cord and rousing goosebumps on her exposed skin. She searched his bold bronzed profile, only to be taken aback by the harsh lines of tension underscoring his spectacularly strong bone structure.

'I don't know what you're talking about,' she whispered apologetically.

Nik thrust open the drawing room door and went to pour them both a drink. In silence he extended a pure orange to her and she grasped the moisture-beaded glass of juice tightly, unable to take her attention off him.

'Didn't it ever occur to you that I was a little off the wall sometimes?' he framed with sardonic bite.

Without responding, Betsy watched him toss back a brandy and registered the strain he was striving to control.

'Well?' he prompted grimly.

'You're a little different…occasionally,' she acknowledged reluctantly, thinking of the wedding proposal that had come out of nowhere and the reconciliation he had chosen not to discuss before moving back in. 'But nothing I can't handle or live with—'

'Let's see if you can work it out for yourself,' Nik framed with dark, driven derision, a muscle jerking taut at the corner of his unsmiling mouth. 'I'm no good at empathy. I find it hard to know what someone is thinking. I instinctively distrust most people. On the plus side, I don't play games in relationships. Even so, my flaws have caused me endless problems in the field of personal relationships.'

Betsy was in a daze. Her head started to thump with the onset of a tension headache because what he was trying to tell her was so much more important than anything she could have foreseen.

'As a child, I was brutalised by a severe level of

abuse,' Nik admitted gruffly, watching her with his beautiful green eyes as if he was suddenly expecting her to start screaming or shouting at him. 'My mother was the perpetrator—'

'Your...*mother?*' Betsy exclaimed in horror.

'My mother...yes—women can be violent too,' Nik extended grittily. 'I've always suspected she had some kind of personality disorder. Whatever, she was very violent. She never wanted a child in the first instance and, worst of all, I reminded her of Gaetano, whom she hated. She believed my father had made a fool of her by getting Cristo's mother pregnant as well and she focused her hatred and resentment on me because I resembled him.'

Betsy was dizzy with shock. 'I had no idea, Nik. Why didn't you ever tell me about this? Those nightmares you used to suffer—?'

'Childhood memories... I also began suffering from flashbacks of the abuse,' Nik confessed in a raw, reluctant undertone. 'It takes me longer to understand emotional stuff...like tonight with Cristo. I went into meltdown because I was very angry and upset. I felt betrayed. I was afraid that you might have developed feelings you shouldn't have where he was concerned, feelings you couldn't acknowledge because you knew you shouldn't have them. I wondered how the hell I would ever get to the real truth and believe it in such a situation...because difficult as it would be for anyone in that position, it's even worse for me.'

'Oh, Nik...' Betsy breathed painfully, her heart going out to him because so much that she had never understood about him was finally falling into place for her.

This was why he struggled when she hurled angry accusations at him, fell silent and brooded when she began to talk about feelings, and ultimately it was why he had misunderstood how she felt about him and walked out on their marriage. He had genuinely thought she didn't love him any more, that she had told him the literal truth. He couldn't comfortably assess such a confrontation and sometimes, regrettably, people threw wild, wounding insults and made threatening announcements purely to shock when they were hurt and angry. After all, that was exactly what she had done with him.

'And this is what I would have done anything to avoid,' Nik admitted angrily, throwing his proud dark head high. 'I never wanted you to know and to think less of me—'

'I don't think less—' she argued in dismay.

'I didn't want you to see me as being damaged and I don't want your sympathy or your pity now,' Nik told her curtly, pale beneath his bronzed skin as he stared back at her in challenge. 'You thought I was perfect and I *wanted* so badly to be perfect for you. I wanted you to look up to me, to respect me—'

'I still do, for goodness' sake!' Betsy swore in passionate rebuttal of his obvious concern. 'You're ten times cleverer than I am and a brilliant, highly successful businessman. Of course I respect you and I could never think less of you. In fact I probably think more of you because you've chosen to struggle very bravely in silence… Why is that? I appreciate the macho aspect of hiding what you deem to be a weakness, but why couldn't you tell me years ago? I mean, for goodness' sake, we were *married!*'

'I was taught always to hide it from people, the bruises, the scars. I became an expert at redirecting people away from my pain and suffering. My own mother saw me as a freak because I would never react to the abuse she put me through. I learnt quickly that if I did react, or cry, or beg her to stop, it would only be worse for me. So I stopped crying, stopped feeling and closed off from her and everyone else completely,' Nik volunteered in the most shockingly calm voice as though his mother's attitude to him had been perfectly understandable. 'She had me in behavioural conditioning sessions by the time I was four years old.'

Betsy studied him in horror but clamped her lips shut on an exclamation that would have revealed her true feelings. He didn't want to hear that her heart was breaking on his behalf. Evidently his childhood had been an endurance test of unkindness and pain. His mother hadn't nurtured or loved him; she had called him a freak. From an early age he had been forced into self-reliance, a fact that could only have increased his innate distrust of others and his isolation.

Emboldened by her lack of embarrassing reaction to his admission, Nik continued doggedly, determined to tell her everything now that he had started. 'Helena despised me. It was bad enough that she had a baby she didn't want but she was ashamed of me too.'

Tears stung Betsy's eyes but she kept her eyes wide, determined not to let him see them. She couldn't bear to think of what his childhood must have been like. By all accounts, his mother had been a less than loving parent and he must have felt that was his fault because he wasn't good enough for her, wasn't perfect. How confused and lost he must often have felt when he didn't understand, she reflected in positive anguish at the thought of the unhappiness he must have suffered.

'My mother was physically abusive,' Nik admitted curtly. 'But the nightmares only began shortly after I met you. I had suppressed all the memories of her cruelty—it was my way of coping. I hadn't forgotten what she did to me. I just didn't want to dwell on the memories. But when I met you I opened myself up to feeling things for the first time and then without any warning I started suffering flashbacks and nightmares about the violence.'

Betsy sucked in oxygen like a drowning swimmer and then she simply couldn't contain her feelings any longer. She crossed the distance between them and wrapped her arms round his lean, powerful body as though she would never let him go. 'You should never have allowed your mother to come to our wedding,' she condemned for want of anything better to say, fearful of revealing her sympathy and damaging his pride, for she was painfully aware that such honesty, such soul-baring, had to be very tough for so reserved and secretive a male. 'Why didn't your grandfather protect you?'

'We lived in an entirely separate wing of his home. He never saw or heard anything suspicious and he assumed I picked up the bruises being bullied at school because I wasn't very good at playing with the other children,' he explained wryly.

Betsy rested her brow against his shirtfront, the solid, reassuring thump of his heartbeat thrumming against her and his warmth sinking into her chilled bones like an addictive drug. 'Why didn't you tell him what your mother was doing to you?'

'I thought I deserved it for not being the son she wanted.'

Her hands linking round his waist, Betsy swallowed so hard that she hurt her throat. He was a man of steel forged in fire and she had never truly appreciated that. He was tough because he had had to be tough to survive, hard because he knew that weakness meant vulnerability and distrustful because too many people had let him down.

'The abuse I suffered is the reason why I chose to have a vasectomy,' Nik spelled out in a harsh undertone. 'I didn't want to have a child in case I too felt the same way my mother felt about me. I couldn't bear to put a child through the same pain as I had suffered. However, I know that I am not like my mother and I decided that the vasectomy was an overreaction on my part.'

His explanation was so simple and yet it rocked her where she stood for it had really never occurred to her that Nik might have had a very good reason to make that choice while he was still so young. She had thought only of more selfish and less present-able motivations relating to reluctance to have his freedom curtailed by the responsibility of becom-ing a parent. She pressed her rounded tummy to his big, powerful frame and leant against him. 'You are a kind and caring man. I know that you will protect and cherish these babies with your life. You are noth-ing like your mother—don't ever think you are,' she breathed shakily.

Nik closed his hand to her chin and tipped up her face to look down at her. 'I was scared that when I told you the truth you would hate me for having got you pregnant—'

'I could never hate you,' Betsy whispered, wide azure eyes locked to his lean, darkly beautiful fea-tures. 'I love you too much for that and I'll love our children the same way…'

His level black brows pleated, his stunning eyes glittering with surprise and curiosity below a fringe of luxuriant black lashes. 'You're saying you still love me? How is that possible?'

'I never stopped. When I said you'd killed my love the day I threw you out, I was being a drama queen,' Betsy confided guiltily. 'I was angry but I didn't mean it—'

'Don't say stuff like that to me,' Nik advised, long brown fingers cradling her delicate jawbone. 'I thought I'd lost you for ever. I went to see a therapist about the flashbacks and nightmares when they got worse,' he admitted gruffly. 'Being honest about my childhood lightened the load and helped me come to terms with it as an adult. I put it behind me. I just don't look back…except where you're concerned.'

'And why am I different?' Betsy prompted intently.

'Because you've always inspired feelings inside me that nobody else does,' Nik confessed. 'But I didn't realise what they were until it was almost too late. I know you weren't happy when we were first married, but *I* was. Just having you in my life and my home was enough for me. Without you, everything went to hell and I was hopelessly unhappy.'

Betsy rested up against him with a sigh of pleasure. 'It was the same for me. I think we belong together.'

'And I think missing you and wanting you and needing you all the time means that I love you,' Nik confessed in a tone of self-derision. 'I'm sorry it took me so long to work out that you make me happy but at least I got there in the end—'

Betsy gazed up at him with wonder in her eyes. 'You *love* me?'

'Without you there's nothing to look forward to,' Nik admitted baldly. 'Even the sound of your voice on the phone lifts me…'

Happiness foamed up inside Betsy, banishing the pain, the worry, the insecurity, and opening up a view of the future that was gloriously inviting. 'I was really scared that you only came back to me to give our marriage another chance because I was pregnant.'

'That was only my excuse. The truth is that I wanted to come back and once I got the idea in my head I couldn't wait to do it,' he confided, looking at her with tender appreciation. 'I can't face my life without you in it.'

Betsy pushed her face into his throat, breathing in the familiar scent of him with huge satisfaction, knowing he was finally home with her in every way. 'Will Cristo ever forgive you for what happened to-night?'

'We've made our peace. He knows he was in the wrong.'

Betsy studied him in dismay. 'That's *not* what—'

'He shouldn't have had any feelings for you at all and he knows it,' Nik parried stubbornly.

'I'm tired,' she whispered, briefly resting her heavy head down on his shoulder. 'Let's go to bed before it gets any later.'

In the hall, Nik lifted her up to carry her upstairs.

'You don't need to do that any more,' she reminded him gently.

'Carrying you gives me a kick, *latria mou*.' Nik laid her down on their bed and a charismatic smile flashed across his wide, sensual mouth. 'And when one of you becomes three and the babies are born, life will be even better because I'll have two extra people to take care of.'

'And we'll all be very demanding,' Betsy forecast in warning as he unzipped her gown and helped her to take it off.

'I love you enough to put up with anything you care to throw at me, *pethi mou*,' Nik asserted, sliding into bed beside her to reach for her slight body and ease her close. 'I think I must have fallen for you the very first time I saw you because I couldn't get you out of my mind.'

Her pale fingers skated lovingly through his silky black hair as she relaxed into the circle of his arms. 'It was mutual,' Betsy confirmed drowsily, winding her arms round his neck. 'I need to get up and take my make-up off. Don't let me fall asleep...'

But Nik was much too content holding his sleeping wife to wake her up. Wide awake, he luxuriated in his wonderfully new sense of peace and contentment. Betsy stirred and snuggled into him with a faint sigh of satisfaction as even in sleep he was the source of her security. In the darkness, Nik smiled. *This,* he was convinced, was the essence of being happy...

Baby giggles filled the air as Nik chased his twin daughters across the beach. 'Come back here!' he yelled, finally acknowledging defeat.

From the picnic rug, Betsy waved baby cups of juice and Dido and Ione hurried back to claim them, little toddler legs moving fast and confidently. In the sunlight the diamond-studded eternity ring that Nik had presented her with when they became parents glittered on her wedding finger. Their daughters were almost two years old now and full of spirit. They were identical twins, rejoicing in black curls, olive skin and their mother's blue eyes.

Rolling his eyes at the ease with which Betsy had contrived to recall the two little girls, Nik folded his long, lithe sun-bronzed body fluidly down on the rug beside his wife. 'Why don't they do what I tell them to?' he demanded.

'You spoil them and you never tell them off,' Betsy pointed out as the toddlers arrived to claim their cups and drink thirstily from the plastic spouts.

Nik studied his daughters with a frown. If only he didn't adore them, if only they didn't remind him of Betsy at every turn, it would have been easier to play the disciplinarian. But the girls had inherited Betsy's eyes and cuteness as well as her sense of mischief. Being a father was both more enjoyable and more demanding than he had expected but he wouldn't have exchanged a day of their often chaotic, busy life for a day without their children.

Whenever they had a few days free they flew out to Vesos to stay at the villa and spend time together as a family. The girls loved the beach while Betsy simply enjoyed relaxing and having Nik all to herself. Nik rarely left Lavender Hall now for more than three days at a time. He had rigorously cut back on his business trips abroad. That lifestyle change had begun when Betsy was still pregnant because he hadn't wanted to leave her, and had continued after the twins' birth when he had soon realised that he wanted to be as fully involved in their daughters' lives as Betsy was.

While the girls munched sandwiches, Betsy watched Nik's lean, darkly handsome face soften as he appraised his daughters. She had never dreamt that she could be as happy as Nik had made her. With no secrets left between them and a great deal of love and mutual understanding, their lives had changed for the better, becoming richer and more absorbing. They still saw a lot of Belle and Cristo and the half-siblings the other couple had adopted. Thankfully, Nik and Cristo's confrontation had not left lingering bad feelings on either side and the brothers were as close as ever. Sometimes they all got together to fly out to Zarif's fantastically opulent palace and enjoy the desert sunshine. But more than anything else, Nik enjoyed being a father and enjoyed being at home.

Of course, not everything between them had been perfect, Betsy acknowledged wryly. Once Nik had appreciated the size of the business operation she was running at the back of their home he had been taken aback and had insisted that the farm shop and its attendant outlets be moved to another site. There had been several heated arguments on that score before that move finally took place to a neighbouring farm that Nik had purchased for the purpose. Now it took Betsy time to drive to work but she had had to concede that with access to the new site lying off a busy main road, business had increased exponentially. Thanks to his business acumen, Nik could really not be bettered as an invariably silent partner.

When they had all finished eating lunch, their daughters' nanny came down to the beach to collect the toddlers and led them back up to the villa for their afternoon nap.

'Adult time,' Nik sighed with rich satisfaction, rolling over with alacrity to stare down at Betsy, who was sunbathing in a red bikini composed of three small triangles. 'How long will it take you to remove that?'

'I'm not taking it off. We could be seen from a passing fishing boat,' Betsy pointed out, her cheeks warming at the thought and the risk.

Nik laughed out loud and tugged wickedly at the tie on the bikini bra to loosen it while stealing her breath with a hungry demanding kiss that made her toes curl shamelessly. 'You may be beautiful and amazing but you can be a complete prude, Mrs Christakis—'

'I admit it, but I do love you very much,' Betsy said in her own favour while craving that wide, sexy mouth of his on hers again, fire dancing across her skin as his hand spread across her midriff, his long, elegant fingers tantalisingly close to her breasts.

'I love you too,' Nik husked, emerald-green eyes gleaming with appreciation as he gazed admiringly down at her. 'For ever isn't long enough to be with you.'

He kissed her again and delight and joy flared through her every skin cell. When he untied the bikini briefs she pretended not to notice, but it was a long, long time before they returned to the villa.

* * * * *

#3257 BILLIONAIRE'S SECRET
The Chatsfield
by Chantelle Shaw

Sophie Ashdown must lure tormented soul Nicolo Chatsfield from his family's crumbling estate to attend the shareholders' meeting. A glimmer of hope in the shadows of Nicolo's lonely world, Sophie soon finds herself under the spell of this darkly compelling Chatsfield!

#3258 ZARIF'S CONVENIENT QUEEN
The Legacies of Powerful Men
by Lynne Graham

Prince Zarif al Rastani once broke Ella Gilchrist's heart. For the sake of his country this ex-playboy now needs a bride, so when Ella returns begging for his help to rescue her family from ruin, Zarif has one condition...marriage!

#3259 UNCOVERING HER NINE MONTH SECRET
by Jennie Lucas

One glance from Alejandro, Duke of Alzacar, and I was his. Nine months on, he's found me again. But no matter how my body and my heart react to him, I'll *never* let him take our son away from me....

#3260 UNDONE BY THE SULTAN'S TOUCH
by Caitlin Crews

What would Khaled bin Aziz, Sultan of Jhurat, want with an ordinary girl like Cleo Churchill? She seems to be the convenient bride Khaled needs to unite his warring country, until their marriage unearths a passion that threatens to consume them both!

HPCNM0714RA

#3261 HIS FORBIDDEN DIAMOND
by Susan Stephens

Diamond dynasty heir Tyr Skavanga returns home haunted by the
terrors of war. But one person defies his defenses...the exotically
beautiful and strictly off-limits Princess Jasmina of Kareshi. With
both their reputations at stake, can they resist their undeniable
connection?

#3262 THE ARGENTINIAN'S DEMAND
by Cathy Williams

When Emily Edison resigns, her gorgeous billionaire boss,
Leandro Perez, won't let her off easily. She'll pay the price—two
weeks in paradise at his side! With her family's future at risk, Emily
faces the ultimate choice—duty...or desire?

#3263 TAMING THE NOTORIOUS SICILIAN
The Irresistible Sicilians
by Michelle Smart

Francesco never thought he'd see Hannah Chapman again—a
woman so pure and untouched has no place in his world. But a
newly determined Hannah has one thing left on her to-do list.
And only one gorgeous Sicilian can help her!

#3264 THE ULTIMATE SEDUCTION
The 21st Century Gentleman's Club
by Dani Collins

Behind her mask at Q Virtus's exclusive ball, Tiffany Davis
reveals her true self—a powerful businesswoman with a proposal
for Ryzard Vrbancic. He rejects the deal, but her ruthless
determination makes him eager to seduce from her the one thing
she's not offering....

**YOU CAN FIND MORE INFORMATION ON UPCOMING HARLEQUIN® TITLES,
FREE EXCERPTS AND MORE AT WWW.HARLEQUIN.COM.**

HPCNM0714RB

REQUEST YOUR FREE BOOKS!

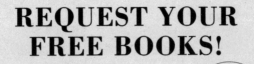

HARLEQUIN *Presents*

PASSION GUARANTEED SEDUCTION

2 FREE NOVELS PLUS
2 FREE GIFTS!

YES! Please send me 2 FREE Harlequin Presents® novels and my 2 FREE gifts (gifts are worth about $10). After receiving them, if I don't wish to receive any more books, I can return the shipping statement marked "cancel." If I don't cancel, I will receive 6 brand-new novels every month and be billed just $4.30 per book in the U.S. or $4.99 per book in Canada. That's a saving of at least 14% off the cover price! It's quite a bargain! Shipping and handling is just 50¢ per book in the U.S. and 75¢ per book in Canada.* I understand that accepting the 2 free books and gifts places me under no obligation to buy anything. I can always return a shipment and cancel at any time. Even if I never buy another book, the two free books and gifts are mine to keep forever.

106/306 HDN FVRK

Name	(PLEASE PRINT)

Address	Apt. #

City	State/Prov.	Zip/Postal Code

Signature (if under 18, a parent or guardian must sign)

Mail to the **Harlequin® Reader Service:**
IN U.S.A.: P.O. Box 1867, Buffalo, NY 14240-1867
IN CANADA: P.O. Box 609, Fort Erie, Ontario L2A 5X3

**Are you a current subscriber to Harlequin Presents books
and want to receive the larger-print edition?
Call 1-800-873-8635 or visit www.ReaderService.com.**

* Terms and prices subject to change without notice. Prices do not include applicable taxes. Sales tax applicable in N.Y. Canadian residents will be charged applicable taxes. Offer not valid in Quebec. This offer is limited to one order per household. Not valid for current subscribers to Harlequin Presents books. All orders subject to credit approval. Credit or debit balances in a customer's account(s) may be offset by any other outstanding balance owed by or to the customer. Please allow 4 to 6 weeks for delivery. Offer available while quantities last.

Your Privacy—The Harlequin® Reader Service is committed to protecting your privacy. Our Privacy Policy is available online at www.ReaderService.com or upon request from the Harlequin Reader Service.

We make a portion of our mailing list available to reputable third parties that offer products we believe may interest you. If you prefer that we not exchange your name with third parties, or if you wish to clarify or modify your communication preferences, please visit us at www.ReaderService.com/consumerchoice or write to us at Harlequin Reader Service Preference Service, P.O. Box 9062, Buffalo, NY 14269. Include your complete name and address.

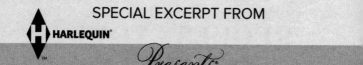
* * *

His expression shuttered, and his dark eyebrows came down into a scowl. "His surname, however…"

I sighed. "I thought you might want to change that. But don't worry." I gave an awkward smile. "I won't hold you to your marriage proposal."

His eyes were dark and intense. "What if I want you to hold me to it?"

My lips parted in shock.

"What?" I said faintly.

His dark eyes challenged mine. "What if I want you to marry me?"

"You don't want to get married. You went on and on about all the women who tried to drag you to the altar. I'm not one of them!"

"I know that now." Leaning his arm across the baby seat, he cupped my cheek. "But for our son's sake, I'm starting to think you and I should be…together."

"Why?"

"Why not?" He gave a sensual smile. "As you said, I already broke one rule. Why not break the other?"

"But what has changed?"

"I'm starting to think…perhaps I can trust you." His eyes met mine. "And I can't forget how it felt to have you in my bed."

Something changed in the air between us. Something primal, dangerous. I felt the warmth of his palm against my skin and held my breath. As the limo drove through the streets of London, memories crackled through me like fire.

I remembered the night we'd conceived Miguel, and all the other hot days of summer, when I'd surrendered to him, body and soul. I trembled, feeling him so close in the backseat of the limo, on the other side of our baby. Every inch of my skin suddenly remembered the hot stroke of Alejandro's fingertips. My mouth was tingling, aching….

"That's not a good reason to marry someone. Especially for you. If I said yes, you'd regret it. You'd blame me. Claim that I'd only done it to be a rich duchess."

He slowly shook his head. "I think," he said quietly, "you might be the one woman who truly doesn't care about that. And it would be best for our son. So what is your answer?"

* * *

What will Lena Carlisle do when pushed to her limits
by the notorious Duke of Alzacar?

Find out in
UNCOVERING HER NINE MONTH SECRET
August 2014